ABOUT THE AUTHOR

Born in Rotterdam in 1931, Janwillem Van de Wetering
embarked at the age of nineteen on a philosophical quest
that spanned thirteen years. His journey took him from
South Africa to South America to Australia before ending
finally in a Buddhist monastery in Kyoto. His first two books,
The Empty Mirror and *A Glimpse of Nothingness*, describe
his experiences with Zen Buddhism in Japan and later in
America. He is also the author of eight mysteries, including
Outsider in Amsterdam, *The Japanese Corpse*, and *The
Maine Massacre*, which was widely praised. The author cur-
rently lives with his wife in Maine.

Books by Janwillem van de Wetering

Corpse on the Dike
Death of a Hawker
The Empty Mirror
A Glimpse of Nothingness
The Japanese Corpse
The Maine Massacre
The Mind-Murders
Outsider in Amsterdam
Tumbleweed

Published by POCKET BOOKS/WASHINGTON SQUARE PRESS

Most Pocket Books are available at special quantity discounts for bulk purchases for sales promotions, premiums or fund raising. Special books or book excerpts can also be created to fit specific needs.

For details write the office of the Vice President of Special Markets, Pocket Books, 1230 Avenue of the Americas, New York, New York 10020.

Janwillem van de Wetering
The Mind-Murders

PUBLISHED BY POCKET BOOKS NEW YORK

POCKET BOOKS, a Simon & Schuster division of
GULF & WESTERN CORPORATION
1230 Avenue of the Americas, New York, N.Y. 10020

Copyright © 1981 by Janwillem van de Wetering

Published by arrangement with Houghton Mifflin Company
Library of Congress Catalog Card Number: 80-26138

ISBN: 0-671-43765-8

First Pocket Books printing February, 1983

10 9 8 7 6 5 4 3 2 1

POCKET and colophon are registered trademarks
of Simon & Schuster.

Printed in the U.S.A.

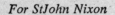

For StJohn Nixon

PART I

1

It was Friday night and the lush heat of summer hung under a clear and starry sky. An old model Volkswagen, dented and rusty on the edges, hesitated before entering the bridge crossing the Emperorscanal at the side of the Brewerscanal. An ordinary car, containing two ordinary men.

Perhaps not too ordinary; the driver had been called handsome, mostly by women, and some of that quality could be seen even through the dirty window that the sergeant was in the process of winding down, unveiling such currently acceptable features as a straight nose above a sweeping mustache, soft, expressive eyes, and thick, carefully combed curls.

"Doesn't work!" Rinus de Gier said. The sergeant, employed by the Amsterdam Municipal Police, criminal investigation department, and veteran of the murder brigade, turned to address his superior. "That window doesn't work. It worked yesterday. Since then you drove the car. You forced it again."

"Yes," Adjutant Grijpstra said, "you're right. Whatever I touch malfunctions. Now drive on."

De Gier concentrated on Grijpstra's face, trying to determine the validity and seriousness of the order. He smiled. The adjutant looked peaceful and solid in the dignity of his crumpled pinstripe suit; a father figure, ten years older than the sergeant who, having passed forty, was aging himself. Grijpstra's body attitude showed what he was: a man of substance, substance of the spiritual variety, an experienced officer,* trustworthy, matured while grumpily serving the abstract state, committed to uphold order so that its millions of wayward citizens could carry on in their egocentric ways. Grijpstra's grizzled heavy head remained impassive under de Gier's scrutiny, but his pale blue eyes reflected restrained impatience.

"Drive on," Grijpstra said, kindly but insistently.

De Gier observed the growing crowd milling about on the bridge. He appraised the crowd's nature and nodded approvingly. He subsequently studied the row of gabled houses displaying their seventeenth-century splendor through the branches of majestic elms lining both canals.

"A lovely spot, Grijpstra. This, I believe, is one of the better locations of the inner city. We are surrounded by decorative and beautiful architecture."

Grijpstra slipped his watch off his wrist and dangled it in front of de Gier's eyes. "It's past ten-thirty, sergeant. We are overdue at Headquarters. The job is done and we aren't working this weekend. The weekend has started."

---

* The ranks of the Dutch municipal police are constable, constable first class, sergeant, adjutant, inspector, chief inspector, commissaris, and chief constable.

De Gier didn't respond. Grijpstra sighed.

"We don't have to be here, Rinus, we have to be in a pub. We should be ordering our first drink. You could be telling me a story and I could be listening to you."

De Gier pointed at a café ahead, a little to the right. It occupied the lower story of a proud and delicate building, and its sign, the goal of the sergeant's long and straight index finger, proclaimed BEELEMA in elegant script; the word was surrounded by a garland of iron leaves.

"I haven't been to Beelema's for years, but I believe that it still attracts an intelligent clientele."

Grijpstra's calm persisted, but the wrinkles around his eyes moved.

"Beer!" he said slowly. "But I won't have it there, and you can't have any. It makes you linger near trees and I get tired of waiting for you. I'll buy you a jenever. Let's go."

De Gier's gaze slipped back to the crowd. The crowd had doubled in the last few moments and began to obstruct the quay.

"Go!" Grijpstra's elbow prodded de Gier's sensitive side. "This has nothing to do with us. Crowds are for the uniformed police. They're here. See? Their car is parked behind that truck, and there's a constable. He can take care of this. He's an excellent constable. His name is Ketchup. He's of the local station."

De Gier, after a swift glance at the adjutant's face, decided to play for time.

"Ketchup?" he asked politely.

Grijpstra tried to wave the question away.

"Yes. The constable has a somewhat violent reputation, he has been known to occasionally bloody a suspect. His mate is of the same caliber, fellow by the name of Karate. Rough maybe, but you can expect it in this area. Ketchup has been talking into his radio, he must have called for assistance. For the last time, sergeant, let's get away while we still can."

De Gier's even but slightly protruding teeth flashed. He parked the car and got out. "Half a minute, adjutant, I'll be right back."

"Evening," Ketchup said. "Did you hear my radio call for assistance? Quick service, sergeant. I know you. Do you remember that evening on the range the other night? When Karate won all the prizes? Pity that Headquarters couldn't win, but we get more practice, I suppose. You were on the team too, I believe."

"I was?"

"Oh yes. Karate is a real crack shot of course, a winner, but right now he's having a bit of trouble. He's in the canal. He's trying to save a drowning man who prefers to drown." Ketchup had to shout the last part of his sentence. The crowd's enthusiasm was increasing. "Goal!" the crowd shouted. "Hurrah!"

De Gier shouldered his way to the bridge. The blue uniform of the swimming policeman contrasted nicely with the deep green color of the slimy and fertile surface of the canal; then the courageous constable became invisible for a moment, as he dived to avoid the splashing attack of the drowning man's stick.

The stick was a crutch. The sergeant addressed Ketchup who had followed him to the railing.

"Is that civilian an invalid?"

"He is, sergeant."

Ketchup smiled eagerly. He was a small man, and de Gier bent down to address his subordinate.

"Explain!"

Ketchup obeyed, immediately and subserviently. Most of his report was lost in the assorted noise produced by the crowd. De Gier frowned.

"Tell me," the sergeant bellowed, "how did this start?"

Ketchup tried to step away, but the crowd pushed him back against the sergeant's chest. He repeated his narrative, shouting, abbreviating his sentences.

"Aha." De Gier had heard. He now fitted the facts together. Karate and Ketchup, driver and observer in a patrol car, were ordered to investigate a disturbance. A street seller, dispensing raw herring and onions from his stall, had telephoned his complaint to Headquarters. Hippies, so the herringman said, were interfering with his trade. The patrol car, delayed by heavy traffic and slowed by many neatly fenced areas where streets were being repaired, arrived late. The herringstall was closed, and there were no hippies in sight. The constables, disappointed, did not return to their car. The evening, so far, was uneventful, and they would welcome some action. Insisting on locating disorder, they were attracted by sounds coming from café Beelema. The sounds were of breaking glass and raised voices. They charged the café. Karate, who led the charge, was hit by a crutch wielded by a drunk.

The sergeant cupped his hands and aimed his shout at Ketchup's forehead. "So you felt threatened?"

"Right, sergeant!"

"And you removed the threat by depositing your man in the Emperorscanal?"

"Right! So that we could create a temporary point of rest. There were other troublemakers: a fat man dressed in leather, a male model in his nighties, and a younger female who yelled. They supported the crutch-clubber. They were ringleaders. There was a dog."

"It attacked you?"

"It growled."

De Gier observed the policeman in the canal, popping up in various places. He shrugged. "You didn't go for your guns?"

Ketchup smiled politely. "No."

The drowning man renewed his attack. His crutch hit the spot that had held Karate's head. The crowd approved. "Olé!"

"Please sergeant, assist Karate. I'll discipline the crowd." Ketchup had found a hole; he slipped away.

De Gier began to undress. He removed the silk scarf from his tapered shirt and looked around. Grijpstra approached and held up his arm. De Gier deposited the scarf. He took off his jacket. He slipped out of the straps that held the gun holstered under his armpit. He stepped out of his trousers. A girl pushed Grijpstra away and admired the stripping sergeant. The girl's girlfriend also pushed Grijpstra.

"Lovely," the first girl said.

"Ooh-ooh!" the second girl said and repeated her statement while de Gier displayed his wide shoulders, his long and muscled back, his narrow waist, and his straight legs.

"The legs are too thin," the first girl said, "not that I mind. Nice, eh?"

The second girl stuck to her original observation. The first girl nudged her.

"Yes," the second girl said, "I like his eyes too, and his curls. Let's wait for him afterward and ask if he is for hire."

De Gier stepped over the railing, hesitated, and jumped. While he jumped he thought it was a pity. The case was not out of the ordinary: a drunk in a canal, it might not happen every day but it certainly happened every week. He had, when he spotted the disturbance, hoped for a little more. He needed work to fill the emptiness of the coming weekend. He saw, while he fell (the mind is fast), an aphorism neatly lettered on the slow green swell of the canal's surface. *Emptiness is the devil's headpillow.* Then a word changed. Emptiness is the *smoker's* headpillow. Not having anything to do for two empty days would surely make him smoke again. He hadn't smoked for five days now. The threatening peace and horrifying quiet of the weekend ahead would break his effort. The weekend would destroy him unless *splash!* The splash exploded both aphorism and reflection. (The mind may be fast, but still moves within time.) De Gier, excused from the duty to think, experienced the sensations of becoming wet and dirty. A condom curled itself around his toe, a soggy newspaper brushed past his mouth, his wrists were linked by a pale green waterweed. He muttered and shook off the condom. The newspaper floated on. He broke the waterweed. He determined his position. His body had turned while it fell, and he no longer saw the constable and the civilian but a row of legs belonging to an orderly line of spectators settled on a tree, felled by age and lying across the canal. The eyes of the spectators were hostile. De Gier breathed out; the rippling water rose to his mouth.

"Watch out!" shouted Karate.

De Gier turned and saw a blond head and a pink hand. The enemy watched him from bloodshot eyes. His spluttering mouth blew a bubble, a balloon that had to be more than mere spittle-film, for it didn't burst, managed to detach itself from the man's extended lips, and wafted away. The crutch was raised, ready to come down, and de Gier spread his arms and propelled himself backward. The crutch came down and shot up again. De Gier's rowing arms provided more distance.

Grijpstra had seen enough. Hindered by jostling bodies and deafened by rough voices the adjutant struggled, liberated himself, and found an abandoned handcart chained to a tree well away from the disturbance.

He climbed the cart, careful not to tip it, and admired the view—a perfect square bordered by bridge, quaysides, and the tumbled elm tree—the arena where the law fought its formidable opponent. He averted his eyes. The view might be interesting but he didn't enjoy its irregular motion. He preferred what lay beyond its limits and observed calm water supporting two black geese with fiery red and bulbous beaks, and glittering eyes. Grijpstra thought that he recognized the scene and searched his memory for associations. The requested information appeared promptly. He saw clearly remembered paintings, created by Melchior Hondecoeter, a medieval artist inspired by birds. The adjutant saw pheasants in a snow-covered cemetery, a giant woodcock defending itself with swollen purple throat and half-raised wings against the attack of jealous peacocks, and sooty coots landing on a castle pond surrounded by crumbling moss-grown walls. He nodded, but Hondecoeter had forgotten to portray these exotic geese, floating in arrogant glory on a green swell of luminous water mirroring steeply rising silver-gray mansions, holding on to each other in their great age.

Grijpstra looked up. The narrow gable frames supported golden balls flanking a stonework angel raising his trumpet. The tall trees, carrying heavy loads of leaves, reached for the angel. The adjutant sighed. He would like to do this painting himself, and perhaps he could, but he would need some rest and unlittered space. His small apartment offered neither. He thought of his flat-footed heavy wife and the overflow of furniture, stacked under low ceilings, in a haze of kitchen smells.

He was ready to sigh again, when the rocking cart forced him into a lopsided dance. An old woman climbed the cart, an ugly shape topped by a glistening skull spotted by transparent clusters of gray trailing hair. She peered at him from watery eyes pressed by puffy skinbags. Her teeth clacked as she spoke.

"Isn't it terrible? Yes, it's terrible. That's my neighbor, Frits Fortune. He doesn't do nothing. It's no sin to be drunk. I order more beer and Frits goes to get it and falls. His crutch gets away and breaks the glasses. We jump about, me and the others, to get hold of Frits and save the drink and down he goes again. The fuzz rushes in. It beats us with nightsticks. Frits gets off the floor and his crutch hits the fuzz, right on the smacker. Accident, everybody knows he don't mean it, but the fuzz knows nothing. They drag Frits out and dump him in the canal. We're friends so we put in a word. I did, and Zhaver, he's the barman, and Titania, she's the barmaid, and Borry Beelema, he's the boss, he also runs the hair salon on the other side. Borry always helps, he does, God's other son we call him, you know? So Borry, he grabs a bottle and *hey hey* we all shout and back comes the fuzz. Then we do nothing, for the fuzz has guns." She waved a claw.

"Yes ma'm," Grijpstra said.

The claw pointed. "I'll be the death of him, poor feller, and all by mistake. Because Uncle Harry got scared of the weirdoes. Calls the fuzz and goes home. You know Uncle Harry?"

"No ma'm."

"Sells herring, he's all right. But when he's in his stall he can't get away and the weirdoes come and yell in his face. Got weak nerves, Uncle Harry has. The weirdoes are on junk, they're needlers, that's the worst. It's terrible, ain't it?"

Grijpstra agreed.

The woman clacked her teeth cheerfully. She faced the adjutant and admired his pink clean cheeks sagging heavily over solid jawbones. Eager to increase her contact, she thumped him on the thigh. The cart wobbled.

"Easy, ma'm."

"Yeh. Poor Frits, he don't earn it, not after the other trouble he don't. Like Job, he lost it all."

"Job?"

"Come on," she said coyly. "You're from my time, you read the Bible. Like *Job,* on the shitheap, man who got boils. Lost everything, right? Poor overnight, and sick too, ain't that terrible?"

"Yes ma'm. Mr. Fortune lost it all too?"

"Yeh. Yesterday. Just imagine, he comes home, worked all day, poor man is tired, a good man, opens the door, and *nothing there.*"

"Nothing at all?"

"Nothing. Over there. See Hotel Oberon? Next door. Old warehouse they changed into apartments. He lives on top and I'm underneath. That's how I know. Frits comes home, puts his key in, opens the door and *nothing there.*"

"Thieves?"

She squeaked like a bird in fear. "Never. His own wife. Never surprised me. Rea Fortune, the silly bitch. Frits's too good for a silly bitch. The mister works while the missus sits on her sucker, if nobody holds it for her, that is. When he's home she yells at him, the floor is thick but I can still hear her. He makes the money and she spends it, but she can't do nothing."

"Mrs. Fortune wasn't home?"

The woman cackled. "Not home? Nothing was home. He gets inside and there's nothing but polished floors. That's why he's got the crutch. He slips and hurts himself. I hear it and I go up and help him down the stairs, take him to the doctor. He's in pain. He's lame. Poor Frits. But she'd taken it all, except the phone, can you believe it? Even the dog is gone, nice dog, a poodle, Babette. But Babette comes back late last night, scratching and barking and Frits lets it in and this morning the dog is gone again, ain't that terrible? So I take Frits to the pub and everybody knows and they all buy him a drink and look at it now."

Grijpstra looked and nodded. Righteous power was closing in; Frits Fortune's movements became restricted by the sergeant's and Karate's strategy. The crutch still swung but it had lost both strength and direction. The sight didn't thrill the adjutant. He averted his gaze and admired the geese again. The birds, ungainly as they climbed a board attached to a houseboat, were being fed by a holy-looking old man. Grijpstra no longer concentrated; his mind reverted to duty. He visualized a report and phrased the essential statement: *While removing all household goods.*

"Mrs. Fortune didn't leave a note?"

"Nothing. She leaves space."

"Nobody saw a van?"

"Nobody. Poor Frits goes about asking, but it's busy here during the day, there's always a van somewhere. Nobody notices. He phones his relatives, everybody he knows. Me too, but I am out most of that day."

"Grijpstra!" shouted de Gier.

"Here."

Fortune was pushed up by the sergeant and Karate. Grijpstra left his cart and received the suspect. Ketchup drove the patrol car alongside. The crowd approached and was restrained by other policemen pouring out of a minibus. Frits Fortune, relieved at being on dry ground again and encouraged by friendly faces in the crowd, whacked Ketchup on his cap. The crowd howled and Grijpstra joined his colleagues and addressed the hostile civilians lovingly, benevolently, touching softly.

"You're fuzz too!" the old woman shrieked.

"Yes ma'm."

"Take care of poor Frits."

"We will," Ketchup said. "We'll bounce him up and down in the drunks' cell and he can roll in his own filth all night. And if he doesn't call us 'sir' tomorrow, we'll have him for a little while longer."

Grijpstra put an arm around Ketchup's shoulders and walked him away.

"Monkeyface."

"Beg pardon, adjutant."

"I say you're a monkeyface. You shouldn't be throwing invalids into the canal. And you shouldn't be fighting in pubs. When there's pub trouble, you should stay in the open door and wait till it calms down, and then you should go in. Don't you learn that at school anymore?"

"Yes, adjutant, but tonight it was different. Karate was a bit nervous and so was I. We wanted to take care of it quickly."

"You didn't. You aggravated and provoked. I'll be mentioning the matter. I'm telling you now so that you know what's ahead."

"Yes, adjutant."

"Take care of poor Frits."

"Yes, adjutant."

De Gier had dressed. "Strange suspect, you know. Blew bubbles. Like bubble gum, but it wasn't."

"The man was disturbed." Grijpstra passed on his information.

De Gier listened while he dried his hair with his scarf. "Yes? Doesn't sound right to me."

"Doesn't sound right at all," Grijpstra said, "but they can explain it in the café, and pour us a drink meanwhile."

De Gier shook his scarf.

"I don't want to drink, I want to smoke."

"They'll have nicotine."

"Like in cigarettes?"

"Of course, and like in shag tobacco, and like in cigars."

"But I stopped smoking."

Grijpstra entered the pub. De Gier stood and watched a cyclist. The cyclist was a slender but hairy gentleman dressed in a three-piece summer suit complete with an old-fashioned felt hat. The cycle was new but a bent pedal touched the metal chain guard, clanging monotonously. Ducks, awakened by the melancholy repetitive sounds, quacked sleepily. The two red-beaked geese honked briefly. The old man who had been feeding them cleared his throat sadly. A shiny Mercedes, parked in front of the Hotel Oberon which occupied the five finest gable houses on the other side of the canal, emitted a fat man.

Grijpstra came out of the pub again and grabbed the sergeant by the arm, turned him round, and pushed him to the pub.

"I read it somewhere," Grijpstra said, "in a book that gives examples of correct reports, based on true cases: *A gentleman lost his temper because his wife annoyed him. He picked up a vase and broke it on her head, killing her. The body rolled on the carpet and bled profusely. The gentleman rolled the body into the carpet and dug a large hole in his garden. He dropped the bundle into the hole, covered it up with earth, and stated: 'My wife has left me, I don't know where she went.'"

"Yes," de Gier said, "and in that way he hid both body and the traces of his crime. I remember the report, but it only mentioned a carpet, not everything that goes into a house. This case is different."

"Every case is different, principles are often identical."

"True."

"We're closed," the barman said. He was dressed in bib overalls made out of imitation silk. Downy hair flowed over the bib. His profile was Greek and divine but no longer young.

"Police."

The barman read the two plastic-coated identity cards and noted the stamps, the photographs, and the diagonal red, white, and blue stripes. He put them on the counter and moved his thumb so that they slid toward a short elderly man who was sitting at the bar. "More of the same, Borry."

The man studied the cards and returned them to the detectives. He felt his stomach bulging under a leather waistcoat, pulled his curly sideburns, and smiled convincingly.

"Drinks on the house, gentlemen. My name is Borry Beelema. I own this establishment, and my hair salon across the water is at your service should you wish to look better than you do now. Titania, ask my friends what they would have."

A young woman presented herself behind the bar.

"Titania?" asked Grijpstra.

"Titania, at your service. What would our guests like to imbibe? A triple whisky with a drop of cognac? Ice and whipped cream? A gilded straw? Please state your desires."

Grijpstra's lips twisted.

"Not that sort of desire," the girl said primly.

"Two jenevers, miss."

Grijpstra turned to de Gier. The sergeant offered no support. He wasn't looking at Titania but at the half-revealed upper part of a young lady on a poster.

Grijpstra corrected his observation. De Gier was looking at the young lady's hand. The hand held a cigarette.

De Gier cursed.

"Beg pardon?"

De Gier smiled brightly. "Nothing, adjutant. I was
thinking. Please proceed."

2

"I regret that I have to state that the tradition of the police, born in a noble past, stretching to an enlightened future, does not allow . . ."

"Yes," Sergeant Jurriaans said softly.

". . . for a shoddy present. Two of your men, dressed in the Queen's uniform, disgraced the force last night. I'm here to complain."

"So I gather."

The two men leaned toward each other across a worn counter in the front office of the police station in the inner city. Grijpstra wore his usual crumpled three-piece pinstripe that now contrasted sadly with Sergeant Jurriaans's impeccable uniform. Grijpstra sighed and prepared to match the power of this tall and wide-shouldered colleague and to withstand the steady gaze directed at him from a heavily lined face under a wealth of cropped orange hair.

"Would you like some coffee?" a female constable

asked. Grijpstra now sighed with pleasure. He noted that the young constable was well shaped and looked back at him through unusually large and sparkling blue eyes. She was small and slender, but her breasts seemed to exert considerable pressure against the stiff material of her jacket. The intensity of her eyes disconcerted him, however, and he faced the sergeant again. The sergeant was rubbing his face. The stiff hairs on the back of his hand reminded Grijpstra of carrot scrapings.

"Please, dear," Jurriaans said, "and I don't mind if you serve the Revenging Angel too. He's a colleague, after all, and carries a superior rank, and he's probably been sent, he can't help himself."

The girl giggled. The adjutant attempted to ignore her. He couldn't. He saw more in her eyes than he wanted to see. Wise, Grijpstra thought, and lewd. She knows it all. How can she know it all? She's too young.

The constable left, gracefully wobbling her small tight bottom.

"Don't mind her," Sergeant Jurriaans said, "she's amused by older men. She likes them, too. She has a father complex. When you get through with your heavy words, I'll tell you a story about her. It's about time we exchanged the news of the day, we don't see each other much lately."

Grijpstra's eyes were on the girl again. Sergeant Jurriaans coughed politely.

"Ah yes," Grijpstra said. "She's as nice from the rear as the front. Why don't we ever get female assistants? Cardozo doesn't compare with . . . what's her name?"

"Asta."

"Asta. And I haven't been sent, Jurriaans, as you know."

"I know. What happened?"

"Two of your constables, Ketchup and Karate, threw an invalid into the Emperorscanal last night. A dangerous crowd had to be restrained by six uniformed colleagues, my sergeant, and myself. My sergeant even had to swim. An unnecessary and painful commotion. Unreasonable, too. Your constables provoked the trouble. There was no charge against the invalid. There'll probably be a charge against him now. If so, I demand that you withdraw it, apologize to the civilian, and take disciplinary action against the constables."

The sergeant nodded. "Right. But the blame is mine. Not just for this but for everything. I admit it freely so that we can continue on our various paths. Do you know why I should be blamed?"

"Tell me," Grijpstra said and stirred the coffee in his paper cup, handed to him by Asta whose attractiveness he didn't notice this time. He removed the plastic spoon and stuck it into the sergeant's cup. The sergeant held Grijpstra's spoon together with his own and stirred too. Then he removed both spoons and inserted them in Grijpstra's cup. Grijpstra took them out, held them in his hand for a while, and dropped them into a trash can.

Jurriaans smiled. "I won that one. Your turn. But first I'll tell you why the guilt is mine for anything that goes wrong, here and everywhere. It has to do with my birth. I could have slipped back but I did not. By making that initial choice I became part of an unacceptable situation which, and not in my innocence I assure you, I accepted. On that fateful moment I became loaded with universal guilt."

"Quite."

"With that out of the way, I will leave the general for the particular. I am also responsible for the system that channels new blood into the force. You still follow me?"

Grijpstra smiled noncommittally.

"I'm with you."

"Do you know how the system works, now, I mean?"

Grijpstra's smile froze.

"No, because you and I started at the same time, but I'm of the uniformed branch and closer to ground level. I know what goes on now and remember what it used to be like. In our days, a commissaris blew some cigar smoke into your face and if you didn't drop—they weren't really corrupt as you'll recall, they smoked whatever the civilians gave them—you were accepted. It was a strong test, but honest. Now it's different. The aspiring cadet is faced by a psychologist, with a degree from a respected university and a violent facial tic, smoking a pipe that doesn't draw in a small room where flies crash into the window. He has to answer questions that the psychologist reads to him from a form that also lists the correct replies. Sometimes the psychologist also reads the replies."

"What sort of questions?"

"About hobbies. Does the young man have hobbies? The reply should be 'growing flowers' or 'jigsaw-puzzling,' but our fellow doesn't know that yet, so, in his ignorance, he states that he likes to beat people. The psychologist knows what to do. He says, 'Hee hee, I won't write that down, sir, you're joking, of course, but I'll mark down, further along, that you have a sense of humor, and that's something else that is needed in the police force today; the right answer is . . .' What did I say it was just now?"

"Composing poetry."

"Right. So the psychologist helps the fellow along and says, 'You do like making poems, don't you?' and the fellow says, 'I sure do,' and the psychologist says, 'Let's hear some of your art, sir,' and the fellow recites,

Swishing swiftly through the sky
for crown and church, I fly . . .

and the psychologist says; 'Right, right, no more, sir, not in this dismal little room with the flies banging against the window and my pipe poisoning the already polluted air. My, you are a sensitive one, the police should be proud to welcome you. What sports do you prefer?' "

"Shooting dolls," Grijpstra said, "with poisoned arrows."

"Exactly, and the psychologist checks his form, shakes his head, chokes, and finally whispers, 'Balls, sir, balls!' and the fellow doesn't understand right away and shouts, 'What do you mean, what do you mean?' and the psychologist gets up and begins to dribble across the room, pretending to catch and throw balls and in the end the new fellow says, after he has said just about everything, they can get really involved you know, sometimes there are fist fights or they break up the furniture, but in the end the fellow catches on and says that he plays a lot of football, badminton, rugby, pelota, jokari, volleyball, squash, tennis, and so on, and the psychologist puts a lot of v's on his form, for he's a mental cripple and can only work a few hours a day and it's time to go home. So they get to the final question and he asks if the fellow ever dreams about the Queen and the fellow gets that one and says he does."

"So he misses a lot of time at school, but he gets through the year, and they put him in uniform and send him to you," Grijpstra said.

"And what do I do with him? Shoot two holes in

his body and file him? Or do I keep him in the refrigerator behind the beer?"

"No."

"I don't do that, I'm glad he came; and I'm glad you came too, adjutant, this is a bad day, and I need a friend. I take the young blighter and I send him on patrol, that's what I do, damn my rotten soul if I don't. I know that he's going to add to the mess, but never mind, out he goes. I've got to be grateful after all, the fellow could have gone on welfare, but he has those ideas about the crown and the church, and the sky, and so forth, and he does dream about the Queen. The colonial attitude, somewhat scarce these days. 'To work,' I say. 'Catch me an invalid and dump the useless son-of-a-whore in the Emperorscanal.' Karate and Ketchup, eh? Who else? I knew it straightaway. Even the marrow in their spines is bad, although they look okay in a way, the despicable little clowns. Asta, darling! See if you can find Karate and his mate. Tell them they are wanted at the counter and don't breathe a word about what has been going on here."

The girl rushed off.

"Morning, sergeant."

"Same to you, Ketchup, and yourself, Karate. Do you know who this officer is?"

Ketchup came to attention, Karate answered the question.

"Adjutant Grijpstra, sergeant. He assisted us last night when we were faced by a hostile gathering and engaged in arresting a troublesome suspect. He and Sergeant de Gier. Assistance to colleagues, sergeant. The operation was successful and the report is on your desk."

Jurriaans bowed so that he could look under Karate's cap.

"Yes, successful." The vein halving his forehead

swelled and crinkled up to the hairline. "Is it true that the two of you dashed into café Beelema last night? Nightsticks at the ready?"

"Yes, sergeant."

"And that you, without warning, engaged in a battle with civilians?"

"Yes, sergeant."

"And that you, in the aforementioned establishment, grabbed hold of an invalid, a man who moves along with the help of a crutch, dragged the said individual outside, and threw him into the canal?"

"Yes, sergeant."

Sergeant Jurriaans lifted part of the counter, walked through the opening, and carefully took hold of one ear of each constable. He pulled in opposing directions. The constables pulled back and squeaked. "Eee-ee-ee-ee."

"Louder."

"Eee-ee-ee-ee."

"I won't have this any longer. I won't warn you two again. The next bleeder you introduce into this station, the next suspect who has difficulty walking, the next civilian who doesn't look altogether healthy and happy—do you know what that arrest will do for you?"

"Eee-ee-ee-ee?"

"It will mean a transfer to a certain little village of fishermen that I won't mention, because the whole building may crash down on us if I do. And do you know what those God-fearing fishermen do with constables who haven't learned the meaning of the word *proportion?*"

"Eee?"

"How they treat those officials who have no idea of *human relations?*"

"Eee?"

"How they approach ignorant policemen who cannot *weigh* this against that?"

"Eee?"

"They grind them to dolls' shit. Ground, sieved, purified, refined dolls' shit."

Sergeant Jurriaans let go. The constables tumbled away and came to rest against opposite walls.

"Did I hurt you?"

"Yes, sergeant!"

"Do you wish to apply for sick leave?"

"No, sergeant."

"You may go to the canteen. The brothel on the other side of the street delivered some apple pie, because we haven't interfered with it for the last five years. Madame baked the pies with her own puffy hands. Sometimes all this becomes too much for me. She sent her two prize whores to carry the basket; the handle was decorated with a plastic rose."

"I want some pie too," Grijpstra said.

"Be my guest, and tell me more. Something jolly this time. Tell me about some nice murder."

"Yes," Grijpstra said a little later, before plunging his fork. "A murder, you said. But I can't tell you much about it yet. It's not the right sort of murder, you see."

"Is there a right sort of murder?"

"Oh yes."

"What's wrong with this one?"

"No corpse."

"No," Sergeant Jurriaans said when Grijpstra had finished his story and three helpings of pie. "A murder because some furniture disappeared? And some silly poodle? And a wayward wife? Don't you have anything better to do? You've got a whole weekend ahead of you and the weather happens to be fine. Go fishing. Or count tits on the beach. Another two miles of beach have been set aside for the naked. I can give you directions."

"No."

"You've been doing something wrong, or you are jumping to conclusions. Is superstar de Gier in this too? How is our hero? He caused a few laughs at the range the other night. I always thought he was supposed to be a reasonable shot."

"You fellows gave him a pistol with the sights out of whack. He's doing badly. Nervous, Jurriaans, very. Stopped smoking and lives in pure insanity. Of course he is in this with me, it's my duty to keep him busy. I'm not expecting him to be useful but he can look at Titania while I work. That's a nice girl, although your Asta is better. What's the use of beauty without invitation? Your Asta is friendlier. Do you ever go to café Beelema?"

Jurriaans grinned. "Sure, and I know Titania. Did you happen to look at her sideways?"

Grijpstra ate his last crumb and scraped his plate. "Yes. That blouse must have been specially designed, and they placed the bottles on a high shelf so that she has to reach up all the time. Whoever cut the armholes in that blouse should be decorated. She does have perfect breasts, doesn't she? Never saw anything like it. Sure, on photographs, but that's all tricks. They photograph them upside down or attach nylon threads to their nipples and pull. Titania doesn't need any of that. De Gier thought so too. We changed places a few times so that we could check the other side. Perfect, Jurriaans, perfect."

Jurriaans pursed his lips. "Not quite. Asta looks better."

"Yes? How do you know?"

"How do you think? I told you she has a father complex and I'm the right type for her. I live a strict life, of course, the police is housed in glass; but pressure is pressure, and there are limits, Grijpstra. I could tell you stories."

"Any more apple pie?" asked Grijpstra.

"No."

"Go ahead then."

"Just one story. Some weeks ago. My wife was watching a program I didn't like and we had an argument. I'm a pleasant man, but there are songs I have heard before, they're all the same anyway. So I left the house. There are evenings you're ready for anything and you should stay home. I couldn't stay home for there were those songs. I went to café Beelema, it's the best place around here. I drank a bit but there was nobody there I wanted to be with, until Asta came in, she lives close by. She wears an old T-shirt and no bra when she is out of uniform. She's beautiful, Grijpstra, I tell you she's beautiful. I said hello and she came to sit at my table. I don't know what was the matter with the girl. She was stone cold sober, but she was all over me. Under the table mostly. Beelema is busy on Saturday nights and nobody noticed much but I wanted to get away. She wouldn't let me. She said she likes older men. I got so nervous I had more to drink. She got on my lap and got my hand under her shirt. Wow, Grijpstra, *wow!* I couldn't stand it and I left and she came with me. She has an old car and we went for a drive. She said she had a friend somewhere in the country, a rich divorced woman who gets lonely at times. Dame by the name of Magda. Good-looking, she said. Thirtyish or so. I didn't care, she was bending over and kissing me while she drove, didn't worry much about stoplights. I stopped worrying too. That car is the biggest mess you've ever seen, outside and inside. Half the stuff she owns must be in that car. She kept pushing it aside to reach for me. We got to some town, I can't remember which one, and it was a nice evening and there was a garden party. She stopped and we went inside, didn't know anybody there but it didn't seem to matter. Next thing she's stripping on a table, with a hundred men ogling her. Heavenly body, Grijpstra, moves right, too. She didn't have much on, so it didn't take long to take it off. Pity in a way. I thought I had lost her, but she came back to me and we were on our way again. She driving with her shirt off, breaking the speed limit. We were drinking in the car; if the state cops had stopped us, well, never mind."

Jurriaans, overcome by memory and emotion, pushed at a crumb.

"Yes?"

"Where was I?"

"They didn't get you."

"Who?"

"The state cops."

"No. We got to this Magda, or whatever her name was. The lady was asleep but seemed overjoyed to see us. Broke out the champagne. Served us in a tight black dress that was mostly transparent. I saw it all, even when she wasn't standing with the light behind her. She suggested a game on the Oriental rug in the living room."

"So?" Grijpstra was whispering too. He was leaning across the table. Jurriaans straightened up. "So nothing. The game started, but I don't know how it finished. I woke up eight hours later on that damned rug. Asta and Magda were having breakfast on the porch. I was sick; Asta took me to the bathroom and home afterward. I missed it. Maybe they did it together."

Grijpstra gaped, then frowned. "Yes?"

"That's it."

"No ending?"

"I just told you the ending. You don't think I would go out with that girl again, do you? My wife only talks to me since yesterday. That particular evening spent itself a week ago."

"Tell me another story with a better ending."

Jurriaans raised his voice to a normal level. "No. These are working hours. You tell me about your possible murder, and about what you did since your theory got away with you."

"De Gier and I visited Beelema's last night as part of our preliminary investigation as to the whereabouts of Rea Fortune, wife of the suspect we found in the canal."

"Ha."

"She's missing, isn't she?" Grijpstra asked.

Jurriaans shrugged. "She is not. She isn't home but what does that mean? There have been some lifestyle changes you know; married women sometimes leave their homes without asking permission."

"While removing all household goods?"

"So what? Maybe it makes it special but not very special. You still haven't got a case. What does de Gier think about your theory?"

Grijpstra gestured. "Not much, but de Gier is never impressed by subtle reasoning."

"He consents to going ahead?"

"Of course. He's a simple sergeant and I'm an adjutant. I'm telling him what to do. He wants to work, he can't sit still in his present predicament. That's why he wouldn't come in with me. He's outside somewhere, watching tobacconists' windows."

"A murder," Sergeant Jurriaans said. "All right. I'm a simple sergeant too and I can't see your view; you have an elevated position. But I would think that you need serious suspicions. I learned that when I still learned. Nobody can be designated as a suspect without serious suspicions that the person has committed a crime. You don't have any."

Grijpstra grunted. "No? If a lady disappears, suddenly and without leaving a note, *while all household goods are removed*—that's a nice clause, I'm keeping it for my report—then I have serious suspicions."

"No," Jurriaans said.

"No what?"

"It's not a nice clause. Household goods are pots and pans. You're talking about everything, including the thing that keeps the door from slamming against the wall and the chromium nut that prevents the toilet-paper bar from slipping."

"You know better words?"

"All contents of the house."

"Thanks."

"See? I'm quite willing to help you. I can help you too, for I know the suspect."

"Because you've got him in your dungeon here?" Grijpstra asked.

"No, I let him go this morning, with a sermon. But I've known him for years. I know the other actors on your stage too. I've been around for a while, adjutant, the environment is familiar to me and café Beelema is where I go when the universal guilt becomes too much to carry."

"You know," Grijpstra said slowly, "when I hear that a woman has gone completely, and that nobody, except one particular person, has the slightest idea where she may have gone to, if such knowledge comes to me and I notice that the husband of the lady behaves in a most unusual manner . . ."

"What do you mean, unusual?"

"What? You weren't there. Frits Fortune didn't just behave strangely, he *mis*behaved. De Gier was trying to save his life . . . I mean, really . . . and the man was actually trying to brain my sergeant with his crutch."

"Man kills wife," said Jurriaans, "it has happened before in my practice. The other day, for instance. Man goes to his work, to some horrible daily drudge, and just before he leaves the apartment, his wife thrusts a verbal barbed dagger in his neck, liberally dipped in poison. The man wheels around, grabs the shrew by the neck, presses and shakes . . ."

"Dead? No!"

"As dead as a doornail. Man drops the body, telephones us and sits in a chair until my constables rush to him. Ketchup and Karate, of course, there happened to be nobody else available. They were throwing up when they came back. Ketchup had to visit the shrink a few times; he kept breaking into tears. That's odd behavior in a police station, I won't put up with it."

"Were you ever tempted to throttle your wife?" Grijpstra asked.

"Sure. Why?"

"Just thought I'd ask."

A slight tenderness moved the lines on Jurriaans's face. "She isn't too bad, and she's beautiful too, much younger than I am. She's been looking for a last fling lately, but she doesn't dare to make the break. Makes things awkward at times."

Grijpstra coughed.

"I don't help much," Jurriaans continued. "I have similar thoughts myself. As you know."

"Right," Grijpstra said. "Didn't mean to pry really. So you let Frits Fortune go. Pity, in a way. After a night in the drunks' cell, suspects interrogate easily."

"True, weakens their defenses. He didn't look in great shape, a little crumpled and his mouth was all dry and caked with filth."

"De Gier says he was blowing peculiar bubbles, like gum bubbles; they flew away."

"Because of the medication. He explained it to me. That's why I let him go. Extraordinary and extenuating circumstances. The doctor prescribed tranquilizers and they don't mix with alcohol. Probably explains his aggression, but this morning he was peaceful. He said he felt fine, wouldn't even take his crutch, didn't limp when he left."

Grijpstra's jaw hardened. "Really? There we go again, the man behaves in a suspicious manner. First he limps and the next morning he runs like a deer."

"That's correct; I watched him leave, nothing the matter with him."

"You said you knew him before. What's he like? Has he ever been in trouble?"

Jurriaans removed a cigar from Grijpstra's breast pocket and lit it. "He owns a warehouse further along the Brewerscanal where he has his business, and he used to live in one of those concrete blocks in the south. He didn't like it there and bought some horizontal property in a remodeled mansion next to the Oberon. Spent a lot of money to get it right and just when he wanted to move in, a bum broke into the place. Fortune came to see me about it, but you know that there's little we can do. The city fathers are socialists and they feel that a bum who finds an empty living place has a right to grab it. Property is theft and all that. The law states that such an act is illegal, but the authorities who employ us feel differently. A ticklish situation and I do what the chief constable tells me to do. He tells me to do nothing, and besides I'm busy, for the police are corrupt and we spend all our time taking bribes from the drug dealers. Right?"

Grijpstra sucked his cigar.

"That's what the papers say we do," Jurriaans said,

"and I've learned not to argue. So I tell Mr. Fortune that regretfully there is nothing I can do to get his bum out of his brand new apartment. But because I know the guy, as I've met him at Beelema's and we've bought each other drinks, I blow into his ear that Beelema is known to be God's other son."

"So Fortune goes to see Beelema."

"He does. Beelema ponders the matter and gives him the address of a certain little pub in a certain little alley where ex–prize fighters meet. But now the fine point of it all. Do you know who the bum was?"

"No."

"Zhaver, the barman at Beelema's. You must have met him last night."

"I met him; lovely looking gent."

"Gent is an understatement. Zhaver is nobility, a count filled with the bluest of bloods, born in a castle that now houses a state committee and its girlfriends."

"You're joking."

"I'm not joking. Xavier Michel d'Ablaing de Batagglia is a count. His father went under with something and didn't come up again, and Zhaver became a bum, a city bum, an Amsterdam city bum, the worst variety. I wouldn't mention what he hasn't done, for it wouldn't be worth the trouble mentioning. But we are the police and we understand that sort of thing."

"Let me see now," Grijpstra said, "pickpocket, drug pushing, prostitution and blackmail, breaking into cars, what else?"

"What else too. He also broke into Fortune's apartment. The turning point in his career, for Zhaver came to see me too, to complain about the ex–prize fighters who threatened to do nasty things to him."

"I can see it," Grijpstra said. "Big lumpy gents with soft voices, one on each side. 'Nice teeth you have, Zhaver,' one of them says and 'Pity they are loose,' says the other, 'we could knock them out in a jiffy, couldn't we, mate?' "

"Those very words. Zhaver drops to his knees, prays and begs for mercy, his tears are cleaning the pavement. 'Please dear bad men, leave my teeth alone.' The teeth stay where they are; Zhaver moves out of the apartment."

"And visits you," Grijpstra said.

"And I see that Zhaver hides some good in his character, but that it won't come out by itself, and that he needs help. I help him."

"Do you help people?"

"Sure, often."

"Why?"

Jurriaans stopped smiling.

"Because it is the task of the police and because I work for the police. I refer you to article 28 of the Police Law. *It is the duty of the police to assist those who are in need of help.* I try to adhere to the law, insofar as the authorities do not restrict me."

"Boy boy boy!" Grijpstra said.

"You want to tell me that I didn't dig that up from the law?"

"You're leaving out the middle piece. I don't recall the exact wording, but that article also tells us that we should maintain order actively. And by *help* the law means that we should help those who have suffered because of some crime perpetrated by another."

"So? Wasn't Zhaver the subject of a crime? Didn't those two gorillas threaten him? And where was our friend supposed to sleep that night? Wouldn't he be stealing or even robbing to obtain the wherewithal to take care of his normal needs?"

"Certainly, but you do go on," Grijpstra said. "You referred the blighter to Beelema knowing that Beelema would refer him to the gorillas. I've never been accused of perspicacity but it does seem to me that you are twisting your argumentation."

Jurriaans took a deep breath. Grijpstra jumped up. "All right, you're nice. Go on. I'm sorry I interrupted."

"And you won't interrupt me again?"

"No."

"You may sit down, adjutant. Zhaver needed help. Also because he is a nobleman. His grandfather burned native villages in the colonies and his father made a mint out of creating work for the unemployed dúring the depression. We have to respect good deeds performed in the past, and a son from a noble family cannot sleep in the gutter."

Grijpstra touched Jurriaans's hand. "How right you are."

"I am. And I thought of how I could save Zhaver. Again I happened to think of Beelema. I went to see him. I had to see him anyway, for a lady visited me here at the station and stated that she had been bothered by a gentleman late one evening in one of the alleys, and her description of the suspect's features and mode of dress reminded me somewhat of Beelema. Borry Beelema is a good man, of course, and God is his father, but he does tend to forget his manners when out for a stroll, and has been known to upset civilians, both male and female, by making certain propositions. The complaints are never too serious as he adheres to certain limits, so we can usually send the complainants home but . . ."

"Beelema, eh?"

"Beelema. And I was upset for another reason. He had given me a bad haircut. Too long. And I felt annoyed for a third reason; another lady had been complaining, bothering us, us the police, as if we don't have enough to do, about Beelema's oversexed dog's forceful behavior. All in all, I was in the proper mood to persuade Beelema . . ."

"The dog!" Grijpstra's hand whacked the table. "You should have seen that dog with de Gier last night. All over the poor sergeant. 'Hello, dog,' the sergeant says, and the animal jumps him and doesn't let go. As if de Gier was the whore of Babylon. The beast went easy at first, but he does know how to quicken his rhythm. Staring into de Gier's eyes too, slime dribbling off his jaws, disgusting, absolutely disgusting!"

Jurriaans grinned. "That's what he does. They say owners and their pets become alike after a while. True in this case, but Beelema isn't as strong as Kiran and the dog's teeth are bigger. Did you manage to liberate your sergeant or did he get the full dose? About half a liter, I would guess; that dog likes to finish what it starts."

"Is that his name? Kiran?"

"Named after a Russian prince, couldn't leave anybody alone either."

"We got him off the sergeant, but everybody had to help. Beelema kicked him out after that, for the dog kept watching the sergeant and slavering."

"So that's what I did," Jurriaans said and frowned impatiently. "Got myself worked up and saw Beelema. I knew he needed somebody to tend bar and Zhaver needed a job and a place to sleep. I'm always happy when the pieces fit. Two or three years ago that was. Zhaver still has the job and he gets on with Borry who has obtained more time to look after his hair salon. Fortune visits Beelema's café regularly; so does his wife, Rea. You want to know about Rea? Analysis of the victim, very important in murder cases it seems."

"Please."

Jurriaans shook his head. "Don't know much about her. I believe she used to be on the stage, long time ago, before she married. A quiet woman, arrogant, talks as if she has a mouthful of hot potatoes. Because she comes from The Hague, I believe they all talk like that out there, but they say that The Hague people are real too. I wouldn't know, I've never been there. You?"

"Once or twice. Attractive?"

"The Hague?" Jurriaans asked.

"No! Rea Fortune, an attractive lady?"

"I wouldn't say so. Not unattractive either. Wishy-washy. I preferred her poodle, a woolly rag with a silk collar, known as Babette. I'll say that for Babette, she knew how to deal with Kiran. One yap from Babette and Kiran was scratching at the door. Admirable behavior, even for an animated needlecraft kit."

"Love and friendship," Grijpstra said, "that's what we see when we want to see it. But in reality there's nothing but evil behind the rosy shades. Zhaver grateful to Beelema, what do *we* know? He probably hates the exploiter's guts and curses him daily from his cramped quarters above the bar."

Jurriaans nodded. "Possibly. He does have the smallest room ever, even smaller than Titania's who lives on the same floor."

"And Zhaver hates Frits Fortune because Frits threatened him through the gorillas," Grijpstra said. "And Zhaver has an affair with Rea Fortune, so has Beelema. Fortune and Titania carry on too."

"Who carries on now? Although you're right that Zhaver isn't gay, he only looks gay. I've given you facts, the rest you can imagine and try to prove. Jealousy is a fact of life, but it isn't always everywhere. I wouldn't follow you in any of your accusations. Fortune, for one, is a fine upstanding specimen. All he ever does is work and when he drinks he only has one or two. Last night was an exception. Personally, I like

them all, except Rea. She can stay away for all I care
and I won't miss Babette either."

Grijpstra got up. "People are no good, Jurriaans.
I don't have to stress the point. If you haven't found
out by now, you should leave the police. I suspect
Fortune of having murdered his wife. Maybe he should
have, but that's the court's business. I plan to pursue
the man. If only I knew what he did with the corpse.
So far, I move in empty space. I don't like that much.
All that emptiness, it's eerie. Bah!" He brought out his
wallet.

"On the house," Jurriaans said. "Come again. Don't
forget to say goodbye to Asta when you leave."

De Gier waited in the street; he was talking to a small
black boy. The boy smoked a cigarette.

"I knew it," the boy said, "but I forgot for a moment. Thank you." He dropped his cigarette stub and
walked away.

Grijpstra touched de Gier's shoulder. "Weren't
preaching, were you? What did that boy know? That
smoking is bad for the health?"

"Wrong conclusion, adjutant. I just managed to
pull that boy from under an oncoming truck and probably saved his life. Whereupon I said, 'Don't you know
that you should look before you cross?' He answered
politely. A nice little boy, even if he happens to be
pitch black."

"You discriminate," Grijpstra said. "So did your
colleague inside, but he was referring to people from
The Hague."

"It's impossible to discriminate against people from
The Hague," de Gier said when they walked to the car.
"Are we going anywhere?"

"To Headquarters. I telephoned the commissaris.

He's making a special trip to his office to hear us. He's got the weekend off."

"I don't want to go. The two of you will be smoking."

"You could smoke too."

"I can't, you know I can't." There was agony in the sergeant's voice and Grijpstra took pity.

"So why did you stop, Rinus?"

"For you."

"*Hondecoeter.*"

"What?"

"Hondecoeter," Grijpstra said. "If you answer out of context, I can do the same. I say *Hondecoeter* and you can find out what I mean."

De Gier drove on silently. He parked in the courtyard of the gray forbidding police building.

When Grijpstra wanted to enter the elevator, de Gier restrained him.

"Now what?"

"I know what you mean by Hondecoeter," de Gier said. "Melchior Hondecoeter was a not-too-well-known painter who liked to portray birds. You took me to see his pictures once, in the municipal museum. They all looked as if they had been painted in the evening. You thought of him last night, when you saw the exotic geese in the canal. I thought of him too. And you mentioned his name because you wanted to draw my attention to the essential beauty of . . ."

"Restrain yourself, sergeant."

"Never mind, don't withdraw at the crucial point. I know exactly what you meant, Grijpstra. You wanted to share your perception with me. Very sweet of you. Really, I'm serious. You're right too, we live in a wonderful world, but we busy ourselves and don't notice."

"I didn't mean anything of the kind."

"Subconsciously," de Gier said. "The true feeling that only comes out in some children and a few artists. I appreciate your true intentions."

"A brothel," Grijpstra said.

"Hey?"

"Apple pie, very tasty. But I would like to know who gets sent to the brothel when there is trouble. There's always trouble in brothels. If he sends Karate and Ketchup, they'll tear the joint apart and he won't get apple pie that way. But he does. So . . ."

De Gier gaped.

"So he sends himself," Grijpstra said triumphantly.

De Gier touched the breast pocket of his shirt. "I forgot to buy cigarettes. I always have cigarettes. Now why did I forget?"

"Sergeant Jurriaans is no good either," Grijpstra said.

3

"What nonsense is this?" the commissaris asked. "It's Saturday. Since when do I work Saturdays? Since when do I work at all? Don't you read newspapers? It says so here, in last night's *Courier*. The *Courier* is writing a regular column on the police these days. It's gotten tired of playing up the drug bribes and now it's paying attention to officers above the rank of inspector. It says that high police officers are only concerned about publicity." He waved the newspaper. "In black and white, read all about it, colleagues. We're stupid too, that was in yesterday's issue. We can't remember the simplest details. So why are you wasting your time with me? Whatever you'll tell me will go into one ear, out of the other." The small old man stood in the dead center of the large Oriental rug that decorated his office. Irregularly shaped orange halberds seemed to grow out of the points of his polished shoes.

De Gier laughed.

"I'm glad I amuse you, sergeant."

De Gier stopped laughing. The commissaris's sharp little nose pointed at the sergeant's forehead.

Grijpstra cleared his throat. "He stopped smoking, sir. His behavior is somewhat irregular."

"Is that so? What's this story on the disappeared household goods? You fellows getting into simple theft? Didn't anybody see the van or truck the criminals used? Trucks don't look as identical as cars; they can be traced without too much footwork."

"No sir. We would like to acquaint you with the framework of our case and ask for your advice and permission to go ahead."

The commissaris almost smiled but snorted instead. "Advice? Permission? Really!" He slapped the newspaper. "Read this. I'm here to beautify the building, and as I don't even do that, I've become an appendix that can painlessly be removed. You two are doing the work. The journalist delved deeply and the quality of his research is admirable. He even took some photographs of my colleagues. You should see how dumb they look. No brains anywhere in their oversize skulls. No function either. Filling rooms on the upper stories of police stations."

"We haven't been able to trace the truck, sir, but we haven't done much so far. The only witnesses we interrogated were people who happened to get in our way. On Monday we can telephone the movers."

"Did you say 'murder' just now, Grijpstra?"

"Yes sir."

"Tell me the story again. You can say something too, sergeant. Do you *have* to stare at me like that?"

"Would you have a match, sir?"

"You stopped smoking, didn't you?"

"To chew, sir."

De Gier chewed. Grijpstra reported. The commissaris dropped his newspaper, picked up a watering can and busied himself with the plants on the windowsills.

"That's all, sir."

The commissaris replaced the can in his cupboard. "Yes, the facts, as described by you, don't tally much. But they fit exactly, of course, once you have the pattern and the other facts. Anything that happens consists of intertwining causes and effects and every single one of them can be traced. Some of your missing facts could be criminal, or they could be harmless. They might very well be harmless. Offhand I would say that Sergeant Jurriaans's approach is correct. Mr. Fortune is having a hard time without you two stepping on his toes. If I tell you to consider him as a suspect he loses some of his liberty, and he has already lost his wife and his possessions."

"And his dog," de Gier said, smiling inanely.

"Job," Grijpstra said.

"Beg pardon, adjutant?"

"I said 'Job,' sir. The old woman who shared the handcart with me called him that. Fortune is Job. Not on the dungheap but in an empty apartment. A comparison, sir."

The commissaris was following the edge of his carpet which contained a number of colored squares. He only stepped on the blue squares which were irregularly placed, so that he had to jump here and there.

"Job. Quite. But Job came out fine. He used the right attitude, passive positivity. The man's faith was impeccable. Hey! You can't be serious, Grijpstra. Are you identifying me with the almighty Father? Are you saying that I have the power to plague the unhappy man further because he'll gain the heavenly kingdom anyway?"

De Gier grabbed his throat and coughed harshly. He spat out a sliver of match wood.

"What now?" the commissaris asked, his voice rising. "Are you okay, sergeant?"

"It's the chewing, sir. Haven't got the habit yet. I shouldn't tear so much; just flattening the match is enough."

Grijpstra was halfway out of his chair. "Please start smoking again, Rinus."

"No."

"A fundamental change of a habitual pattern causes critical effects, adjutant. We'll have to harden ourselves. Job, eh? A most interesting comparison. God and the devil gambling and the suspect is the stake. Let's hope he is intelligent and knows he can't lose. Did I ever tell you about the time that I lost my car?"

De Gier suffered another attack of harsh rasping coughs and it took a few minutes before the commissaris could entertain his assistants. He had, a few years back, been issued a new Citroën of the expensive variety and was pleased with the classy vehicle. He thought of an errand, drove into town, and parked the car. When he returned the car was gone. His disappointment was mingled with fear. Not only that something wasn't there that should be there, not only that the missing item was the gleaming auto he had been so proud of owning a few minutes ago—the loss could be related to events of the past, he had attempted to twist his car key into thin air before—no, the emptiness confronting him at that fearful moment was more than he could have expected. The Citroën wasn't there and the ground on which it had rested wasn't there either. The commissaris, abruptly transformed from acting object into suffering subject, stared down into a gaping hole. The bright red bricks were replaced by a black aperture that sucked at his very existence.

"Then," the commissaris declared, "I doubted the benevolence of the creation and I haven't dared to stop doubting since. Another loss that added, in a way, to my liberation. To lose may be frightening, to know that you have nothing can be encouraging."

"And the car, sir?" Grijpstra asked.

"The car? It returned. There is always a superficial explanation. I forget what had happened exactly, maybe the sewer burst, or a gas pipe. They suddenly had to dig a hole and my car happened to be in the way. I telephoned, and a polite lady told me where they had left the Citroën. But who cares? I'm talking about something else. We don't have earthquakes here, which is a pity. To be reminded that even the ground isn't safe, that we are forever suspended in undefinable space; very heartening, adjutant. To assume that we rest on gravity tends to make us dullish. It must be fun to see the planet sway and bubble and crack up into holes, for then we know where we are, and, presumably, what's to become of us."

Grijpstra looked blank, de Gier tittered.

"Very well, adjutant. Pursue your investigation if it makes you happy, but do try to find some serious suspicions before you trip over yourself and others. And, by the way, has it occurred to you that Rea Fortune may just have left? To get away is legal, you know. It's a right guaranteed by our democratic constitution."

4

"Listen here," Frits Fortune said, "you're really not all that welcome. Why don't you leave?"

The suspect was lying down on his side on an air mattress under the open windows of the largest room in the apartment. De Gier sat opposite him, cross-legged. Grijpstra, unable to find a suitable spot, walked about, becoming visible every now and then through open doors. Fortune still wore the same clothes, a linen suit of good quality, crumpled and stained. He smelled mainly of damp rot but the stench mingled with the fragrances of soap, shampoo, and after-shave. Fortune smoked, spilling ash on the shiny parquet floor.

De Gier admired the glowing cigarette. The pack was within reach of his right hand. It still contained nineteen cigarettes. De Gier wanted to grab it, tear off the paper and silver foil, spread his hand around its entire contents, and light all cigarettes at the same time. He would then inhale the combined smoke into the extreme depths of his lungs. Afterward he would feel better.

"Won't you leave?" Fortune asked again.

"We'd rather not," de Gier said, "but if you insist, we'll have to, for to stay, after having been told to leave by the legal possessor of living space, constitutes a crime and would, in our case, being police officers and having identified ourselves as such, be punishable by a double maximum penalty, or six months in jail. But if we leave, we'll have to return with an order signed by a high-ranking officer. We have a car and it wouldn't take me longer than half an hour to obtain such an order. With a warrant you'll have to admit us, and if you refuse, *you*'ll be punishable."

"But what do you want of me? Is it because of last night? I remember vaguely that I fought with policemen, including yourself. You were in the canal too, but I don't believe you were in uniform."

"I'm a detective."

"You are? I'm sorry if I hurt you with my crutch. Did I hurt you?"

"You only intended to. Any charges the constables may have come up with have been dropped. We aren't here to remind you of last night, we only want to know the whereabouts of your wife."

Fortune rested his head on his arm. "Gone."

"Gone where?"

"Doesn't a detective detect? I've tried, but being an amateur I failed. I could only think of telephoning everybody who knows Rea. I made a list; here it is. It's been in the water too, which hasn't improved my handwriting. I checked off all the names, which means that I telephoned those people. I borrowed the telephone book of my neighbor downstairs, Mrs. Cabbage-Tonto and . . ."

Grijpstra reappeared and held up his hand.

"Is that her name?" de Gier asked. "Cabbage-Tonto?"

"The lady who lives below this apartment?" Grijpstra asked.

"Yes."

"Cabbage-Tonto," Grijpstra said thoughtfully. "The right name. If I had to name her I couldn't do better."

"Of Italian origin and married to a dead Englishman," Fortune said.

"There's always a superficial explanation."

Fortune nodded at the adjutant's disappearing back.

"How . . ." De Gier extended a hand and pushed the pack of cigarettes away. "How is your leg, Mr. Fortune?"

Fortune laughed. He had good teeth. His face was good too. De Gier thought of a hero he had seen in an old war movie that ended well when the bad enemies surrendered and the good flag was raised.

"My leg? My leg is fine. There's nothing ever wrong with me, really, I only have weak nerves. Or I'm crazy, like most of us. Whenever I have a bad fright, a part of my body goes wrong, but only for a while. Some time ago I was nearly run down by a car and I fainted on the sidewalk. The specialists played snooker with me. I hit every hospital and clinic in town. The doctors agreed in the end that I might have a bad heart and that the next severe shock would knock me down again. But they were wrong, as you can see. When the constables hit me and lost me in the canal, I didn't even faint. The shock repaired the effect of a previous unpleasant experience, when I came home to find nothing." He sat up. "By the way, those little constables are dangerous, they should be restrained. The same goes for that fool sergeant Jurriaans who disciplined me this morning. And to think that I've known him for years and respect him in a way. Another Aunt Coba, appearances mean nothing, a black soul in respectable dress. Arrrgh!" He lay down again.

"Aunt Coba?"

"She has been living on the Emperorscanal for several centuries now. As a child I used to spend time in her house; with her and Uncle Henry. A dignified-looking couple but their valor is lopsided. Only Uncle Henry will go to heaven."

"You stayed with them? You're not Amsterdam born?"

"Of course I am, but my parents lived on the other side of the river and my mother was sickly. I would be sent to Aunt Coba. Aunt Coba would interfere with my mind. Would you like to have coffee?"

They went to the kitchen, finding Grijpstra observing an empty shelf. On the stone sink stood a hot plate and a box filled with groceries.

Fortune talked while he made the coffee. "Never thought Rea could be that thorough. She even took the toilet paper, very bothersome if you notice its absence too late. Had to use the paper in my pocket diary, too thin and too slippery.

"Not that the experience isn't two-sided. Without obstructions one can see far. When the dizziness wore off I went shopping. It happened to be Thursday evening and the stores were open. I could even buy a mattress and lie down and think it out. I used to think in a circle, about the business, about money. More of this to get that, more of that to get this."

"You publish books, we were told."

"I certainly do, or did maybe. A good selection, if I say so myself, nothing but what the public wants. Books on how to grow tomatoes in water, and what the gurus say about coitus and meditation, illustrated. Today's subject today, for those who want to live free in the security of togetherness. The cozy seekers, Holland's hope."

De Gier looked for a match. Grijpstra frowned.

"Coitus?" Grijpstra asked. "Meditation? Separate or simultaneous?" He sipped his coffee, didn't like the taste, and continued to frown, studying miniature swells in his plastic cup.

"Both, the book is in two parts, but I don't know too much about the quality of what I sell. A publisher believes in sales and calculates in profit. There's no choice. Expenses increase and profit diminishes. Only more of this gives more of that, as I explained just now."

Grijpstra's frown dissolved.

Fortune smiled. "The endless circle, but not quite, as I found out on the mattress in the other room. To think that I quarreled with Rea because I refused to sell the circle. To consider that someone, a colleague who lives on the next canal, would buy my garbage on behalf of his company—a hundred times the size of mine, he doesn't own it but he's a director—would offer to free me, and I actually refused." He shook his head.

"At the right price?"

"A little more."

"Your wife wanted you to sell?"

"She did and I wouldn't agree. My colleague invited me to dinner at Beelema's, Rea was asked to come too. Borry Beelema likes to serve meals at request. He serves himself, and Zhaver and Titania dress up as cooks. Beelema believes in perfection. Caviar and champagne. Hyme, my colleague, must have discussed every detail of the party. It was meant as a trap, but I hadn't learned yet how to be caught in order to become free. FREE, damn it! They may not have known how to approach me. I'm a quiet man, or used to be. I worked, and that was all. Hyme sidled up along conventional lines and wined and dined me to soften up my resistance."

"The price?" asked Grijpstra.

Fortune told him.

Grijpstra whistled. "You could retire."

"And I didn't want to."

They had left the kitchen and stood alongside each other, gazing out of the windows. Below them a sea of irregular roof tops was contained by a row of warehouses. A thrush, perched on the head of a gargoyle, initiated a fairly complicated statement. The silver Mercedes with the German number plate that de Gier had seen before slithered to a stop before the striped awning of the Hotel Oberon and the same fat German slammed his car door and waddled across the street.

"You refused outright?"

"No, I asked for time to consider the offer. I was alone, under attack by a wicked monstrosity, horribly eager to rob me of my safe routine, or so I thought. I pretended to laugh a lot, became angry, and went home."

"With your wife."

"Yes, then we fought."

"Did you hit her?" Grijpstra asked pleasantly.

"No. I repeated myself. We didn't sleep that night. She wanted to buy a car, a country house, furnish it in style. She said I could read books. I told her that I manufactured books."

"You don't read?"

"I do, but not too often. I told her I was being useful to society. She tore me to pieces. She proved I wasn't, that the other company could publish my trash better than I."

"Was she right?"

"Of course."

Fortune thought.

"You would sell now?" Grijpstra asked.

Fortune grinned. "Yes, I will. I've been looking at my products again. Goat-wool socks, hallucinating mushrooms, UFO wisdom, Mr. Hyme can have it."

"UFOs may exist."

"Sure, but what do my authors know? They know how to spread ignorance on two hundred pages. They fantasize or lie outright and connect nonsense with fabrication."

The thrush sang on.

"Rea was right, but for the wrong reasons," Fortune said. "And she didn't care. I care now, and I disagree with her motivation. All she wanted was wealth, happiness, some short-range goal like that. She's a silly woman really."

"You won't take her back?"

"No."

"Divorce?"

"Yes."

"What will the neighbors say?" Grijpstra asked solemnly.

Fortune lit another cigarette and puffed placidly.

"Mrs. Cabbage-Tonto? She's the only neighbor I know and she never liked Rea. Sure I'll divorce Rea, but she'll have to show up or write to me through her lawyer. I'll return her money to her; she brought a fair sum into the marriage. I invested it in the business. I'll pay her back with profits."

"You're angry with her?"

Fortune dropped down on the mattress.

"No."

"And what do you plan to do?"

Fortune yawned. "Nothing much. Think more out of the circle, right here. This is a good place to think. Go on a trip afterward, find a quiet place, build my own cabin. I can't do that yet, but somebody may teach me."

"Will you have a car?"

"I'll have to learn to drive again. I could when I was in the army, that's twenty years ago. I don't have a license."

"Your wife can't drive either?"

"No."

De Gier swirled his coffee. "The dog, do you think it will come back again?"

"It did come back and I can't understand where it went. I'm sure I locked the door. It's Saturday today, yesterday I was in the canal, Rea left Thursday. I come home and it's all gone. I fall, Mrs. Cabbage takes me to the doctor. I do some shopping. Babette is at the door when I come back, pleased to see me, yapping, affectionate. I go in with the dog. On Friday I leave the dog in the house. It isn't there when I come home."

"The dog could only leave through the door?"

"Door, communal staircase, front door, there's no other way."

De Gier pointed at a wall built out of rough bricks. "Solid wall."

"Yes, the building used to be a warehouse, everything is solid. You see the holes in that wall? I drilled them and drove in cast-iron bars to support my book shelves. She even removed the bars."

"Do you miss your books?"

"Not really. A few perhaps but they can be replaced. Books become stuffing after a while, something to collect; another circle."

"What subjects did you read yourself?"

"Some novels, travel, horror."

"Any particular horror?"

"Poe."

"Poe," Grijpstra said helpfully. "I've heard of him. What's he like?"

De Gier pressed his hand against the wall. "I'll tell you a Poe story. There was a couple. They weren't happy. They lived in the country on an estate. It cost them all they had to keep the estate going. The estate wasn't profitable and the lady couldn't buy what she wanted. She would screech at her husband and one evening he picked up the poker and brained her."

"That was bad," Grijpstra said.

"Not too bad. It solved the squire's problem. But the corpse was still there, he had to remove that as well. Wait, I almost forgot, they also had a cat. The cat was around. Okay. The gentleman was a handy fellow and he got some tools and made a hole in the wall. A big hole, big enough to hold the corpse. He put the corpse in the hole and closed it up again."

"I've never done any masonry," Fortune said.

"But the squire had, you see. He was handy, as I said just now. He did an excellent job. Another thing about this gentleman, he had a sense of humor. He waited a couple of days, a week maybe, and invited the local constable for a glass of wine. Wait, I forgot that cat again. The cat disappeared. The squire looked for the cat but it had gone. Right. The constable comes and gets his wine and the squire pours himself some, too, and tells jokes. After every joke he laughs, loudly, *haha, hoho,* and knocks on the wall with the poker. Harder and harder." De Gier hit the brick wall with his flat hand. "Like this. The squire kept on laughing, *haha, hoho.*" De Gier shouted. A reaction on the roof became audible. There were screeches and cackles, a rustling and a flapping.

"Sea gulls," Grijpstra said.

"And crows," Fortune added. "There are always

crows on the roof, but they are noisier now than usual."

"Let's have a look."

Fortune showed de Gier a trap door and the sergeant stepped into Grijpstra's hand and hoisted himself nimbly through the hole.

"How does that story finish?" Grijpstra asked Fortune. "Or don't you know how it goes?"

"Yes, I know the tale well. When the squire banged the wall with his poker, something inside the wall screeched back at him. An earsplitting screech, unnerving him and the constable. The constable had the wall opened and found the lady's corpse standing up. On her disheveled head sat the cat, the cat that your colleague kept forgetting. The cat was alive, and it screeched."

De Gier's head popped back. "Come up here, I found something."

"A corpse?" Grijpstra asked.

The corpse was on the other side of the roof, partly hidden by a chimney. It had neither ears nor eyes and its skin was badly torn, but it was still recognizable as the remains of a small poodle. Around its neck were the remnants of a red silk collar.

"Babette," whispered Fortune. "Poor little thing. Whatever happened to you?"

Grijpstra sat on his haunches and studied the dog's head. "Got a bit of a blow, the skull is broken. The birds didn't do that, they've only worked on the softer parts of the body."

De Gier walked away until he reached the roof's edge. He looked down and staggered backward.

"I'm nauseous," he said softly, "and dizzy." He held his stomach. "If I don't absorb some nicotine into my blood quickly, I'll lose control. I'll be mumbling and I'll never stop. I'll be gesticulating too. I'll be mentally ill. Maybe they'll let me do something in therapy. I could sweep the path, somewhere in the rear of the asylum, in the cemetery, between the gravestones of the medieval disturbed. Nobody'll come to look for me."

"Talking to me?" Grijpstra asked.

"Yes. I'm telling you that I'm no good as a policeman."

"You never were," Grijpstra said, "or I wouldn't have asked for your transfer to the murder brigade ten years ago. Look at Fortune."

Frits Fortune had cradled Babette's head in his hands and peered into its empty sockets. His pursed lips were whispering endearments. He was also crying.

5

"Now what kind of a man is Frits Fortune?" Grijpstra
asked. "If we don't answer that question, we don't answer anything. Is he a comedian? Is he a nice guy? Is
he a murderer? He could be a nice guy but I think
that he is a murderer."

Grijpstra leaned on the railing of the bridge. De
Gier leaned next to him. A municipal barge, its lone
skipper using the helm as a support for his back, approached slowly through the Brewerscanal. The skipper's legs were spread, he had his hands in his pockets,
and he gazed straight ahead. The bent bodies of the
detectives underwent a slight tension. It could just be
possible that the barge would turn and sail under the
bridge into the Emperorscanal. If it did, it would hit
the elm tree straddling the water. The resulting accident would be spectacular and cause considerable
damage to houseboats. There would be bodies in the
water and appreciable commotion. The all-pervading

silence of a late Saturday afternoon in the inner city, underlined by the monotonous growl of the barge, would be ripped into a thousand shreds.

But the barge didn't turn and the detectives returned to their quiet questioning. The red-beaked geese appeared majestically. The hairy well-dressed cyclist turned up; his pedal still clanged against the chain guard. The shiny Mercedes parked in front of Hotel Oberon and the fat German got out. The door of Café Beelema opened and closed. Kiran, the Great Dane, romped about the quayside, slowed down and left drops on trees and lampposts.

"Stupid dog," de Gier said, "I hope he doesn't see me."

Kiran saw him and barked cheerfully.

"What kind of a man is Frits Fortune?" de Gier asked. "And what kind of question do we have here? Is it the right question? What sort of a man are you? What sort of a man am I? Sometimes I've been known to be like this, at other times, however, I'm more like that."

"This and that are limited ideas," Grijpstra said. "They're the extreme limits that hold the habitual behavior of a suspect. If he did something before, we know that he may do it again. If he was a comedian yesterday, chances are he'll be a comedian today."

"I used to smoke but I don't smoke anymore. What does that make me? A nonsmoker who smoked? A former smoker turned the other way? A nonsmoking former smoker who will smoke again? Finished once, done forever? Once started, on forever?"

"You are a nicotineur," Grijpstra said, "and you have a weak character. But as you aren't a suspect, I don't care what sort of a man you are."

"No?" de Gier asked. He raised his voice. The old

man, feeding the geese on the board attached to his houseboat, looked up. "Shshsh!"

"What sort of a man are you?" shouted de Gier.

The old man crumbled his last piece of bread.

"What sort of a man am I?" he asked in a clear high voice. "I'm a feeder of red-beaked geese. I am what I do and I do what I am." He sprinkled the crumbs like a stingy farmer sowing his field, nodded, and shuffled back into his boat.

Grijpstra laughed. "He's a shuffler-into-boats. And I'm a haver-of-hunger."

Kiran trotted on to the bridge.

"And so is the dog. Care to join us in a visit to a sandwich shop? Or don't you dare?"

Kiran stood against the door, imploring de Gier. The sergeant opened the door. Kiran fell/jumped inside. The dog placed his front paws on a stool and slobbered two meatrolls off the plate of a client. Then he ate another meatroll out of the hand of another client. The clients objected and the dog growled. He stopped growling and embraced a young woman who entered the shop.

The detectives found a booth in the rear. Protected but invisible behind its high partitioning, Grijpstra shouted for service. He shouted twice again before a square woman with a granite face growing from a starched dazzling white coat inquired after the purpose of his powerful exclamations.

"A roll with warm meat, another with chopped steak, another with ox sausage, and another with *two* meatrolls."

"A hundred," the woman said. "Pay now."

"*What?*"

"You let the dog in. The dog stole twenty guilders' worth and is now outside gobbling a liver worth eighty that I had to give him so that he would leave."

"Are you out of your mind?"

"Out," the woman said.

They walked along for some distance, then they walked back.

"If only we could find somebody who knows Fortune well," Grijpstra said. "I could ask Borry Beelema, and the man who tends bar in his nighties, and Titania, but I believe, with the certainty provided by almost total probability, that they are all interchangeable parts of the same thing and not on my side. I need somebody on the outside, which is my side, outside the lost lady and the dead dog but still within the boundaries of the suspect, if such a person existed."

"A relative?" asked de Gier.

They faced the display window of the sandwich shop. Kiran had returned to his opening position and implored the detectives over his shoulder.

"Again," Grijpstra said. "Shall I . . . ?"

"No, he'll be stealing and raping," de Gier said. "He's done it already, we shouldn't allow him to step into the same river twice."

Grijpstra stopped. "I can find him a similar river. A relative you say. An aunt or an uncle?"

"Both. Aunt Coba and Uncle Henry."

"True. I forgot. I'm getting old. Those people live on the Emperorscanal. This is the Emperorscanal. We need a number. You know what, I think I'll open the door for that dog. Like this he looks pitiful. This is not a normal attitude for a dog, he'll get cramps in his paws. Maybe he won't be so hungry for he ate that liver. The girl has gone so there's nothing to rape. He might communicate with the woman who wasn't polite to us and with the big men sitting at the counter. What do you think?"

"The decision is yours. There's a public telephone over there. I'll find Uncle Henry's house number. Let's hope he's a paternal uncle and that his name is Fortune too." De Gier left.

Grijpstra opened the door. Kiran barked and fell/jumped inside. Grijpstra walked on. A slowly passing coach, filled with Japanese tourists being instructed through loudspeakers, drowned a disharmony of sounds erupting from within the restaurant.

6

Aunt Coba smoked a cigarette, Uncle Henry smoked a pipe, Grijpstra smoked a small cigar, and de Gier didn't smoke. The four protagonists sat on armchairs, upholstered with green velvet, on the back porch of a mansion built and kept in an exuberance that would surely have been liberating if Calvinism and the urge to make both spiritual and material profit hadn't imposed certain limits. The open garden doors offered a view of rhododendron bushes gracefully curving around a sea of lowly flowers. A choir of invisible songbirds engaged in a fairly steady melody embellished with trills and twitters. Aunt Coba and Uncle Henry were stately miniatures, and their faces were nicely chiseled by age and determination. They looked alike, under silvery hair cut and combed in identical fashion, and wore about the same clothes. Antique unisex, the sergeant thought, observing and admiring their narrow trousers and flowing jackets of old shiny velours.

Uncle Henry talked around the stem of his pipe.

"Nephew Frits did something wrong?"

"No, Mr. Fortune, not that we know of. But we're looking for his wife, who seems to have disappeared. All household goods, I beg your pardon, the contents of the house, disappeared as well. So did the dog, we retrieved the dog; it was dead, however."

"Still had its head?" Aunt Coba asked.

Grijpstra stared.

Aunt Coba repeated her question loudly, articulating the syllables.

"Yes ma'm. But somebody knocked it on the head. The skull broke. The dog was on the roof."

Aunt Coba nodded happily.

"Never was much good."

"The dog?"

"Nephew Frits. If you *knew* what experiences we had with him! But how could you know?"

Uncle Henry coughed painfully. Aunt Coba's beady eyes pierced her husband's forehead. He coughed again and patted his chest.

"You want a glass of water?"

"No. Isn't it coffee time yet?"

"Not for a long while. Why don't you go and write some checks? You always write checks on Saturdays. I'll take care of these gentlemen."

Uncle Henry didn't move. Aunt Coba's steady gaze increased in strength. He got up, excused himself and left the room.

Aunt Coba sighed. She restrained her hands that were about to rub each other.

"So Rea has gone, has she? Doesn't surprise me, no, not at all. What isn't needed anymore is put away. Such a nice woman too, serving, servile even. And married to Frits!" She sighed again, sadly this time, also a little longer and deeper. "Ah well."

"Yes ma'm."

"But that's the way it had to go. His father was a Fortune and his mother was crazy too. Whenever she got too crazy, the child came here. *Little Frits is going to spend some time with Coba.* She always said that with such conviction. I was never asked whether I wanted to put up with that child, the child just came."

Empathy flooded Grijpstra's face.

"And what would little Frits do, when he stayed with you, ma'm?"

"What wouldn't he do?"

"What wouldn't your nephew do, ma'm?"

"He would wet the bedclothes. He wouldn't eat cauliflower, with or without white sauce, the sauce didn't matter to him. He would use half a roll of toilet paper at a time. If that garden fence was locked, it always was locked, and if he wanted to get his push-bike into the garden, he would break the lock, again and again. He picked his nose, at mealtimes preferably. He didn't do well at school. He stole money."

"Your money, ma'm?"

"No. He stole at home. But he wasn't home much, he was mostly here."

Aunt Coba gazed at the garden. De Gier kicked Grijpstra's ankle, too hard, because his leg jumped out of control. Grijpstra began to get up, but de Gier pushed him back. De Gier's lips formed the word "home."

"What else did he do at home, ma'm?"

"He read. He wasn't allowed to read, the doctor said he shouldn't. He had to play. He was given a box of toy bricks, an electric train, and a teddy bear. He refused to play, although he would pretend to play. He attached strings to the bricks and kicked the string while he read, and meanwhile the train moved around and around. They gave him another train with a clockwork he would have to wind now and then, but he worked out a defense. Do you know what he did with that train?"

"What did he do, ma'm?"

"My sister-in-law came into the room one evening, and there were no lights in the room. The curtains were drawn. Frits had inserted matchheads into the locomotive and the little carts and wagons, and lit them. A big flame rushed around the carpet. It frightened his mother and she tripped over the rail. Half the house burned down."

"Is that it, ma'm?"

Aunt Coba shrank in her armchair. Her eyes glistened behind her gleaming glasses.

"You know what he did with his teddy bear?"

"No ma'm."

"The teddy bear was called Brom. It was a big bear, of good quality and expensive. One day Brom disappeared. Frits's parents couldn't understand what had happened to it, and they didn't trust Frits's peculiar answers to their straightforward questions. Do you know where Brom was found?"

"No ma'm."

"Buried in the garden in a shallow grave. And do you know what else Frits had done?"

"No ma'm."

"He had beheaded Brom."

7

Grijpstra danced. Two little steps ahead, a little step to the right, then to the left, to the rear, and repeat. He sang sidewards and backwards.

"Weedeeho. Weedeeha."

"Don't do that," de Gier said, "or do you want me to dance too? I will if you insist, although I see nothing but misery. What *is* the matter with you?"

"Good luck comes to those who keep on trying," Grijpstra said, performing a fresh set of steps with care, "and whoever insists will win in the end. I've been trying for a long time. So here it comes. A chance encounter, you will say, providing incidental information. In a way you are right, but I see more. Bull's-eye I see, thanking fate meanwhile, and you too. If you hadn't stopped last night . . . I don't want to think about what would have happened then. But you stopped the car, dear friend, and activated yourself and handed me the murderer, solemnly in your inimitable way. You raised him from the water for me to receive and appreciate your gift, decorated with weeds. 'There you are,' you said, and 'thank you kindly,' I replied. And you made your gesture so *naturally.*"

"Are you done?"

"Weedeeho. Weedeeha."

A patrol car rode by with a tall male constable at the wheel and a young female, impeccably uniformed, most of her long dark blond hair tucked away under a small round cap, in the observer's seat. She observed Grijpstra's dance and waved. De Gier waved back.

"Nice girl," de Gier said, "but very young for a constable. I think she knows you."

Grijpstra no longer sang and lowered his foot. He stood.

"Her name is Asta. She's not so nice. She seduces older men. Men like you, sergeant. From forty years old upward. She would even seduce me. Sergeant Jurriaans told me about her. He managed to escape her clutches, but she wounded him, I think."

"Ah."

"Ah what?"

"Interesting," de Gier said.

Grijpstra's heavy forefinger pressed against the sergeant's chest.

"For you perhaps, I will introduce you. If you won't smoke, you can still have Asta. She would be a minimal risk to you, and you would keep her away from others."

De Gier's large brown eyes dreamed away.

"Sparkly eyes," he whispered, "dominating an intellectual face, alive with sensual unfulfilled longing. A good mouth with the fullness of the lower lip restricted in the tight curve of the upper edge." He shrugged. "Too young."

Grijpstra's finger dropped away.

"Let me tell you what Jurriaans had to say about her."

De Gier listened, then nodded.

"Yes, I see. Drunken driving, indecent exposure, adultery, lesbian cavorting. Not all of it is punishable, but he should watch it all the same, and he shouldn't tell you. The relationship still continues?"

"No," Grijpstra said. "She's all yours." The adjutant's voice trailed away. His feet shuffled.

"Please," de Gier said. "Not again." He pointed at a display window. "Look, adjutant, final sale. Just the store for you, elegant and expensive. See that cap? For ten guilders? A gift. But maybe your head is too fat, you think your head is too fat for that classy cap?"

Grijpstra danced into the store. He tried the cap. The fit was a little tight. He left a ten-guilder note near the register and danced out of the store.

"Weedeeho. Weedeeha."

"Please, Grijpstra, that'll be enough. Let's sit on that nice tree over there. You can't dance on it, for you'll fall into the canal. Let's go look at the geese. A moment of peace and quiet, Grijpstra."

De Gier guided the adjutant to the fallen tree. Grijpstra balanced carefully on the fairly wide trunk. De Gier followed. They sat down.

"What happened is clear," Grijpstra said.

"What happened?"

"You described it yourself when we visited the suspect. Frits and Rea are sitting down together, man and wife. Togetherness in the living room, without harmony. A conflict situation about to change into turmoil. Rea Fortune is a woman of fantasy. She pictures herself in a chauffeured Mercedes automatic, silver sheen finish."

De Gier looked up. "The driver is German."

"If you like."

"Fat? Bald? Rolls of bacon for a neck?"

"Whatever your choice, a chauffeur, may I continue?"

"Yes."

"Rea Fortune, she wants to go out. She wants to eat snails in a wine sauce, brought by waiters with Byzantine profiles. A Gypsy plays the violin, right into her ear. High notes, glassy, harp in the background. Fortune said so himself. A woman of fantasy, unfulfilled."

"He gave no details."

"*I* give you details so that you can see how it happened. Unfulfilled fantasy leads to frustration, frustration leads to tension, tension translates itself into deeds. *Mis*deeds. She attacks the suspect, sucks the blood from under his fingernails, chips at the last shred of his discipline. I understand both sides. I'll write some of this into my report. A horrifying circle; woman irritates man, man hides in his habits, he works even harder, reads even more, talks even less, irritates her even more. They'll never go on holidays, they'll never have any fun. She becomes more aggressive. Tension increases, becomes unbearable. The woman shrieks her insults. The poodle yaps. The man's nerves snap. *Bam!* Sometime earlier this week. The poodle escapes into the street, while Fortune gets rid of the household goods, beg pardon, the contents of the house, in a hired van, with the help of a couple of illegal migrants, Pakistanis maybe, Turks maybe. The poodle returns. Fortune is pleased; he takes the animal into the house, tries to enjoy its company, but the dog is whining, it looks for Rea. Again, *bam!* Babette gets chucked onto the roof and becomes dinner for the birds. Bear Brom got buried. Habitual behavioral patterns repeat themselves. But where did Rea go? Oh *no!*"

Grijpstra groaned. He looked about him but didn't

seem to recognize the sergeant or the familiar sur-
roundings.

"Now what?"

"But of course I know where she went. How stupid
of me. Of you too. We could have known it all along.
Amsterdam is a city of holes, fenced-in holes. They're
always tearing at the street bricks, taking them out,
stacking them, digging, fencing, taking the fences down,
filling the holes. Aren't they?"

"He buried her in the street?"

"Where else? He didn't have a car and he couldn't
give her to the Pakistanis or the Turks. Had to keep
her in the house. He looked out of the window and
saw the street workers had been at it again. Holes
everywhere. He picked up the corpse, nipped outside,
buried her, removed the fence. You think the street
workers remember where their holes were? Never. They
just come in the morning and dig and cover up, whatever comes first. But I've got to get that corpse, Rinus,
no corpse, no case. They'll have to tear it all up again."

"You do carry on."

"Hmm?"

"You chatter and prattle. If the commissaris could
hear you, he'd water your neck with his little plastic
can."

"The commissaris would listen politely," Grijpstra
said. "Politely and approvingly."

"Would he now? Think of the base your construction rests on. You're building a tottering tower on the
unconfirmed and hearsay gossip that Frits Fortune, in
the remote past, as a toddler, whopped a teddy bear.
He is, you state, a bear-whopper. I was a smoker. I no
longer am. If somebody asks me, 'Do you smoke?' I
say, 'No, I do not,' and I speak the truth. If somebody
asks Fortune if he is in the habit of whopping bears, he
will reply, 'No, I do not whop bears,' and that can be

the truth too. It doesn't have to be true, but it could be true."

"*You* carry on," Grijpstra said. "You're suffering withdrawal effects. You're a bit out of your head. Not that it matters. I will do this job alone. Stay with me so you'll be safe. I'll provide distraction by keeping you busy."

"There's Kiran."

The dog stood on the quayside and chewed on a cap.

"Haha," Grijpstra said, "he got hold of somebody's cap. Probably took it from one of the fellows in the sandwich shop. Look at that, he's tearing off the rim."

"That's your cap."

Grijpstra felt his head.

"Where's my cap?"

"Probably fell off when you danced onto the tree. Kiran found it. He's got strong teeth, hasn't he?"

"Miserable hound! Hellish mongrel! Is nothing holy in the city of Sodom? Get away, Rinus, I've got to get by you."

De Gier got up. He tried to turn around Grijpstra's bulk. Grijpstra held on to him.

"What goes on there?" two harsh voices inquired. "Get off that tree, you two."

"Sorry, adjutant," Karate said. "Ketchup thought you were fighting. I thought you were fighting too. You weren't fighting, were you?"

"No. There goes Kiran, Rinus. Escaping into Café Beelema. I'm going there too, to ask for immediate compensation. Coming with me?"

"Adjutant," asked Karate, "are we correct in assuming that you left number 33, Emperorscanal, just now?"

"You are," Grijpstra said.

"Were you visiting Mr. and Mrs. Fortune?"

"I was."

"And the man who happened to fall into the canal

last night, by accident so to speak, wasn't his name Fortune too?"

"It was."

"Curious," Karate said. "It's a small world. A while ago, maybe a year ago, Ketchup and I also visited the Fortunes."

"Pleasant people," Grijpstra said, "and reliable too. They supplied me with welcome information. And now I will go to Café Beelema. I want you to arrest that dog. That dog robbed me of my cap and subsequently destroyed it."

"Did you say reliable, adjutant? Did you say that Mr. and Mrs. Fortune supplied you with reliable information?"

"Yes."

"That couple is not reliable, adjutant. That couple is mad."

"Why do you think so, constable?" de Gier asked. "Please explain your reasoning to the adjutant. Don't bother to explain it to me because I'm mad too. But the adjutant's mind is in perfect order and he has to know everything. Especially as he is now working on his own."

8

"We visited the address officially," Karate said, "following orders as we always do. It was about a year ago; I can check the exact date if you like. We were sent by Headquarters, because of a fight, of sorts. It could have been anything, an exchange of words or missiles, but we didn't know what to make of it because of the address, which is good. Ketchup thought there might be a sex club, there are some around here. We'd been to one before; that was because of a fight too. We found naked ladies up to their ankles in broken glassware. So were some of the clients, and one had lost his eye. I found it for him and he lost it again. Amusing in a way, for the time being, that is. Later it turns to work when you have to write it down. We found a variety at that club, and all of it was bad. There was gambling, and liquor without a license, a bit of junk, some weapons, and a minor. All of it to be reported on, but that would be later, as I said. There was a gentleman there who got away without his clothes in an Alfa Romeo. Nervous he was and he drove into the canal; not at once, for the car stuck on the railing. We watched it and thought maybe it wouldn't go all the way, but it did in the end, and the fire brigade got it out. Very nice."

"The damage," Ketchup said. "Unbelievable indeed. Another client in a Porsche, in a bit of a hurry too and didn't look where he was going. Hit a street full of cars on both sides and all the owners pouring out of their houses. You shouldn't laugh and I didn't. It cracked my jaw, it hurt for days. Endless damage!"

"Right," Grijpstra said. "Well, we'll mosey along."

"Wait, adjutant, please, don't interrupt, Ketchup. As I said, we stood on the steps of thirty-three and the old gent opens up and acts all surprised and says, 'Good evening, constable, anything wrong or are you coming to visit the servant?' and I say, 'No sir, we came to ask *you* what is wrong because we hear there is a fight,' and he says, 'No, you must have been given the wrong number, there are some Negroes further along who play the trumpet,' and he wants to close the door, but his wife comes and holds it and tells us that she was expecting us and to please come in."

"So it gets difficult," Ketchup said. "She is pulling and he is pushing. There was a fight but they don't manhandle each other, they manhandle us. What to do? How to write it down? Do conflicting elements constitute a prosecutable misdemeanor or will it be the easy way out again? Are the officers harassed?"

"Just a moment, Ketchup. As I was saying, adjutant, the lady had phoned but it took half an hour before we found out what for. They served us coffee and a spot of cognac, they threw in cigars, although he said she shouldn't. We are busy, he said, and mentioned the trumpeting Negroes again. Then, in the end, she told us what it was. Would we arrest her husband and take him with us, for she was complaining about being threatened with appreciable physical injury. By him."

"Right," Ketchup said, "and that's unlawful. They were married, but even so. Rape is okay but they didn't do that so much anymore. They got to threatening, he threatening her. We were supposed to take action. I spent a while in the bathroom and checked the situation in my notes; I carry notes for special cases. It was right there, clear enough."

"A moment, Ketchup. See what happened, adjutant? He had threatened her and he had done it every night for years. The judge would like that, for it makes it worse. He'd ask for coffee and she wouldn't want to make it and he'd say, 'Right now, dear, away with you, to the kitchen, or I'll knock you down. I'll wring your neck. I'll batter you to death. Get up, dear, I'll count to three.' And he was serious, she said, he'd pull faces, and count and push himself out of his chair and she'd have to rush to the kitchen or he would do all that. But she wouldn't let him do that anymore because of equal rights, and so she phoned Headquarters and here we were."

"What?" Grijpstra asked.

"Yes, adjutant. Thought you might want to know. Not quite what one would expect, although she was right in a way. Knew the correct terms too. If you don't do it, you aren't *in the legal exercise of your service,* she said. I wonder where she found the term, maybe she was hiding in the classroom when I went to police school. And that's what we would be, not in the legal exercise of our service, if we ignored her complaint."

"Go on, constable," de Gier said.

"We arranged matters in the end, sergeant. There was no way we could have arrested old Mr. Fortune. I don't believe you know our Sergeant Jurriaans. If we

had brought that old bird in, he would have pulled our
ears and there'd be *ee-ee* again. We couldn't refuse
either, for she was out for his blood and would have
written to Headquarters. The cognac saved us, and
another two hours of patient listening. Disgraceful in
a way, and Karate got drunk."

"And yourself?"

"Just a little," Ketchup said. "I drove him home.
Karate was tired and he couldn't remember where he
lived."

De Gier looked at Grijpstra.

"Would you care to go?"

Karate and Ketchup saluted. Grijpstra watched the
patrol car drive off. He was whispering and de Gier
leaned close to catch the words.

"Good luck comes to those who keep on trying,"
Grijpstra whispered. "A minor setback. Now I'll find
the corpse." The whisper was fierce and de Gier
stepped back. "I'll find that corpse, sergeant," Grijpstra shouted, "even if I have to lift the last brick in
the last alley!"

De Gier led him away.

"That Sergeant Jurriaans," de Gier said, "maybe
you're right. I don't think he's much good. He tortures
his subordinates and rapes them when they're female.
Didn't you tell me that he made that lovely young cop
strip on a garden table and perform on a carpet with
another lady?"

"You got that wrong."

"Tell me again then."

"It was the girl, Asta, who caused the trouble, not
Sergeant Jurriaans who is a mature man who happened
to be off balance that evening, because of his wife who
is restless and who watches TV."

"Asta," de Gier said softly.

"Stay away, the girl is horse medicine. You might

start smoking again and die peacefully of cancer at a ripe age. That would be better."

"Asta."

"You're not old enough for her," Grijpstra shouted. "She likes older men. Like Sergeant Jurriaans. Like *me*."

"Yes," de Gier said softly. "I'm sure you're right, adjutant. Maybe I shouldn't interfere."

9

De Gier stood in front of Café Beelema. His head rested against a lamppost.

"How do you feel?" Grijpstra asked.

"Constrained. In my throat, spreading to my lungs. Everything is closing up. My veins are narrowing, the blood no longer flows. I would like to shout, or cry perhaps, at the same time, I think. Do you have cigarettes on you?"

"Cigars. There'll be cigarettes in the café. All brands. Shall I get you some?"

"No, I just thought I'd like to know. I don't smoke anymore. I'll stand here for a while. It'll pass and then it'll come again. I'm in a tunnel; I'm a worm, a pink worm, stretched, pulled on both sides. The sensation is painful and hopeless. I suffer, Grijpstra."

"Poor fellow."

De Gier pushed himself away from the lamppost.

"Right. Hell is not forever. There are pauses. Without intermissions there would be no hell. If the experience were continuous, I'd get used to it. This way I can't. I'll suffer again later. Let's go."

They went into the café and greeted Titania who stood behind the bar, Zhaver who was playing with Kiran between the tables, and Borry who sat at the counter. Zhaver pulled on what was left of the cap and Kiran growled.

"That's my cap," Grijpstra said. "That's an evil dog."

Beelema jumped up.

"I'm sorry, adjutant. Let me reimburse you. What did the cap cost you?"

"Ten guilders, but what's money? Paper with figures printed on it. I just bought that cap. I liked it. Look at it now."

Kiran dropped the slimy rag and grinned. Borry put up all his fingers and pointed at the register with his nose. Titania took out a ten-guilder note and gave it to Grijpstra.

"With my apologies, adjutant," Beelema said, "but the dog is still young. A little playful, eh? I'm glad you could find the time to drop in. The city is empty today, everybody has gone to the beach to annoy the tourists. Those of us who remain should keep each other company. Can I offer you a drink?"

"A beer," Grijpstra said and sank down on a bar stool. The beer soaked into his gulping throat. He replaced the empty glass. Titania refilled it. De Gier wandered about. A well-dressed middle-aged man came in and sat down at a table. He picked up the newspaper and glanced at Titania. Zhaver asked the customer what he would like to drink. The man didn't see Zhaver, he stared at Titania. Titania saw him but seemed unaware of his attention. The man put his hands on the table and raised himself slowly. He staggered to the bar. "Hello." His voice croaked. He was pale and his hands trembled.

"Sir?" asked Titania.

"Hello."

Titania looked at Zhaver.

Zhaver asked the man if he was all right. The man let go of the bar rail and began to rub his stomach.

"Yes," he said. "No. Excuse me." He left, swaying slightly. He had trouble with the door handle.

Grijpstra was impressed.

"And your arms were down," he said to Titania. "You're beautiful indeed. You unnerved that man."

"Maybe he was drunk," Beelema said soothingly. "It sometimes happens. We see it happen every now and then."

"They ask for a drink and we give it to them," Zhaver said. "Then they ask for another. They keep on doing it every day. Slowly they turn into alcoholics. It's sad, but that's the way it sometimes goes."

De Gier stood at the window. "He's going into Hotel Oberon."

"They have a bar too," Titania said.

"He's still on his feet, maybe he's all right."

Several tourists entered the café, South Americans, with mustachios and gleaming teeth; they trailed a woman in a low blouse filled with trembling, soft, fertile flesh.

The blouse's contents did not match the Titania's. Titania wasn't doing anything on purpose; she reached up, she had to, the bottles were on a high shelf. The gesture freed her breasts; the mustachioed gentlemen could see everything from the side, and those who were placed farther along the bar, from the other side. A moment is now, and now lasts forever. The gentlemen saw what they saw through narrow appreciative eyes. The lady saw what the gentlemen saw. Her lower lip tightened and her upper lip moved up just a little, but it changed her face. She hissed while she should have swallowed. The liquor burned her throat. The gentlemen beat her on her back while their eyes rested on the Titania's.

Other customers came in and were served by Zhaver.

"Are you working?" Beelema asked.

Grijpstra pushed his glass to Titania. "A little, we have a question. A simple question. Where is Rea Fortune? Answer the question satisfactorily and we'll be free."

"She is gone."

"Yes, yes."

"Don't you believe me?"

"I believe she's gone."

Borry Beelema thought.

De Gier stopped wandering and leaned against the bar. He studied the embroidered shirt of the café owner, the artificial color of his thick, curly, hair-dryer-fluffed sideburns, his golden wrist and neck chains, the well-cut trousers that minimized the bulge of his belly and lengthened his legs. He thought he might find the man's photograph in the police files. He seemed to remember having seen the photograph. Perhaps in the drawer of sexual offenders. What would have been the charge? Shared delight with a minor? Harassing female pedestrians by holding on to these innocent and self-centered beings and, without having been invited, touching, or even kneading, certain of their prominent or hidden parts? Or would it have been the usual display of the pink pecker?

"Rea Fortune has gone," Beelema said, "which is a pity, or isn't it a pity? What do you think, Titania?"

Titania blushed.

"You're blushing," de Gier said. "How becoming. Look, Grijpstra, Titania is blushing."

"Don't," Titania said, "please."

What a lovely closed face the girl has, de Gier thought. Each feature is perfect. Then he forgot what he was looking at. Segments of another face fitted together. This other face was Asta's, but he had only seen her briefly, as she passed him in the patrol car. Yet the face was clear, clearer than Titania's. But what was Asta, apart from Grijpstra's misunderstanding of Sergeant Jurriaans's observations? He concentrated on the tip of Grijpstra's cigar. It smoldered like a pit in a Lilliputian's hell. In the microscopic flames, Asta's face formed itself again. He forced his eyes back to Titania.

"Titania is in love," Beelema said, "with Frits Fortune. It's a drama we have lived with for some time now. Frits Fortune doesn't know what goes on in Titania's heart, because she's a modest girl who resigned herself to the impossibility of her desires. The man was married, wasn't he, and he still is, but Rea has gone, so now the coast is clear."

"Heaven be praised and thanked," said Zhaver, "for we can no longer bear her unhappiness, although we, on our side . . ."

Titania broke into tears. "You dirty . . ." She didn't finish her observation. She ran away. A door slammed. The soles of her shoes rattled on a wooden staircase. Another door slammed.

"That wasn't clever of you, Zhaver," Beelema said. "Now you have to work for two. The gentleman over there has been waiting for service. Why don't you ask him what he wants?"

Zhaver took the fat German's order. The customer wanted two knockwursts on toast with pickles on the side. He also ordered beer. Zhaver dropped the sausages in a pan. Zhaver grumbled.

"What's so dirty about going to bed with Rea? Did you think it was dirty, Borry? You enjoyed it too."

"Did you sleep with Mrs. Fortune?" Grijpstra asked Beelema.

"Now and then."

"Did Mr. Fortune know?"

"I didn't tell him."

"Disgusting."

"There you go," Zhaver said. "She wanted to."

"She was often home alone," Beelema said. "It isn't that bad, is it? Times are freer, you know, and the police are slow to catch up. We did it because we wanted to help. Titania is in love with Fortune. Titania is ours and we fight on her side. Rea didn't even like her husband. A proved point, she ran away, didn't she?"

The German complained, loudly and with a thick accent. He wanted his beer. Beelema brought it to him. He also wanted his knockwurst. Zhaver fished the sausages from the boiling water, popped up the toast, spread the pickles. The German ate, blowing heavily through extended nostrils.

Grijpstra had become busy with sipping his beer, arranging his cigars and his matches on the counter, and moving his bar stool. He found some coasters to be lined up in a square. He studied a number of bottle labels. He scratched the stubble on his chin and felt his navel. In the end he patted the side of his jacket.

The concrete presence of his pistol provided some peace of mind. His body sagged back in the accepting attitude it had assumed before the disturbance of new facts interfering with a theory. Rea Fortune has disappeared, he thought again, as he had thought before forming the theory. Rea Fortune's absence remained the foundation on which all theories would rest. If Rea were there, he, Grijpstra, wouldn't be here, he would be home with his wife and children in the upstairs apartment of the Oilmakerscanal. Streetside view: water displaying floating objects, mainly made of rubber; rear view: windowsills displaying other objects, mainly plates containing scraps of food.

Rea Fortune is not there. Why? Because her husband killed her. Why did he kill her? Because he lost his temper, that's why. Everything thought out and approved, tightly completed. Next step: *find corpse.*

But what if everything changed? If, apart from two new lovers (Rea's), a fallen-in-love girl (with Frits) were added to his collection? How would all this fit the original and tested theory? Grijpstra sweated. His hand dropped and once again patted the textile-hidden pistol. This support did not stop his forehead from sweating. All factual evidence so far obtained danced around the adjutant, including the headless bear Brom and the earless and eyeless Babette, including the lovers and the enamored girl, naked and pornographing.

He left his bar stool, grabbed hold of the wandering de Gier, and pushed him to a corner table.

"I won't pay," the German said loudly. "The beer was warm and the knockwurst was cold."

His statement caused no comment, but the sergeant left his chair and walked to the phone. He dialed, spoke, and returned to the table.

"I'm sorry," Grijpstra said, "I know I've been treating you badly, in a condescending manner, because of your temporary affliction."

The door opened and closed. Two uniformed constables, one male and elderly, one female and young, entered the café. They switched off their electronic communicators and looked at Beelema. Beelema pointed at the German who was staring at his meticulously cleaned plate and empty glass. The girl constable marched up to him.

"You won't pay, sir?"

The German answered her in the affirmative and explained why he had come to his decision.

"You've got to pay, sir."

"I will not."

The elderly constable stood in front of the door, a resigned but heavy presence. He contemplated the floor. Kiran barked and embraced the girl. When he barked again, he was flat on his back in a far corner of the room and appeared to be in pain. The girl resumed her original position. The café became as quiet as before.

The German's eyes, embedded in pale fat, glowed. The girl's eyes sparkled through long lashes. The German took out his wallet, produced a note, and put it on the table.

"Will that be enough?" the girl asked Beelema.

Beelema nodded.

The elderly constable stepped aside. The German waddled through the door. The elderly constable followed him. The girl smiled at de Gier. She saluted. She followed the elderly constable.

"Got to have that corpse," Grijpstra was saying. "And you should help me. Without the corpse there is nothing but vagueness, nothing but . . ."

"A ripped fog in the early morning."

"What?"

De Gier smiled encouragingly.

"A ripped fog in the early morning. I saw that this morning, above the river, when I drove into town. Lovely, but you can't hold on to it. I understand what you are saying, Grijpstra. What a beautiful place this café is. Just look at that paneling, it's rosewood and well joined. Look how Zhaver contrasts against that background of mirrored bottles. Study Kiran, lying on sunlit boards. If I were smoking now, I wouldn't have this awareness. Nicotine narrows the potential of imaginative reception by slowing the blood flow in the brain. It limits the capacity of the senses. I'm close to the essence of creation. I see that everything is glorious indeed. Too glorious in a way, I don't think I can stand it."

"Hold it."

"I will see what I can do for you, Grijpstra. Please tell me how you intend to find that corpse."

"Right. The corpse is close, under the road bricks. But where exactly? I've thought of a method to determine its location. We must have Fortune followed. He will be attracted to the spot where he buried his wife, for marriage creates a link, strengthened in his case by crime. We can't follow him, for he knows us, but he doesn't know Cardozo. Listen carefully while I go into details and tell me what you think."

"No," de Gier said a few minutes later and smiled over Grijpstra's shoulder at the expanse of the Brewers-canal, stretched quietly in the heavy yellow light of the late afternoon.

"I'll do it anyway."

"You won't," de Gier said, "but how did you ever think of it? How wonderful."

Grijpstra inhaled deeply. De Gier cut the adjutant's protest with a loving wave of his arm.

"Not now, Grijpstra, I want to see it again." His eyes rested on the canal's surface while he saw the phantoms raised by Grijpstra. First of all there goes the suspect Fortune, wandering in solitude, a prey to his own bad conscience and his self-inflicted demons. His muffled curses interchange with gnashing of his teeth. At a safe distance follows a detective. He is Cardozo, constable first class, a member of the murder brigade, a small figure, untidy and long haired, blending with the city. He carries a bundle of red flags. Everytime the suspect's behavior changes, whenever Fortune curses or gnashes louder, Cardozo remembers where the change occurred and inserts a flag between the bricks. The flags are small but bright of color and are seen by the laborer who follows the detective. The laborer drives a yellow machine, grumbling on wide crunching tracks, the machine carries a blade, and the blade digs holes. But each hole is always empty.

"Each hole is always empty."

"But where could the corpse be?"

"Each hole is always empty, and how will you defend your decision when you are asked to explain the holes?"

"I do have serious suspicions," Grijpstra said sadly.

"You do not. You have a bizarre construction, resting on what isn't there. You have negatives and you're adding them. No contents of a house, no lady, no life in a dog. Added negatives do not make a positive. You have a no head on a hearsay teddy bear. You have an insufficiency, adjutant, you have a nothing obscured by shapes."

"What can I serve the gentlemen?" Beelema asked. "You're just sitting. You aren't ordering. It's dinnertime. Tell you what? I invite you to come to the sandwich shop with me because my kitchen is closed because Titania is crying upstairs."

"No, no," Grijpstra said. "Can't you send for some food? It's nice here, why leave?"

"Yes," Beelema said, "what will it be?"

"A roll with warm meat, another with chopped steak, another with ox sausage and another with *two* meatrolls."

"Yes," Beelema said, "and the sergeant?"

"A roll with meat salad, another with crab salad,

another with lobster salad, and another with *two* meat-rolls."

"That'll be four meatrolls," Grijpstra said worriedly, "two for him and two for me, that makes four. Not two, not one for him and one for me, but two each, that's four, but only with two rolls, one for him and one for me. Can you remember that?"

"Four each?" Beelema asked. "Isn't that a lot? He doesn't smoke anymore and should be careful and you're heavy already. It isn't my concern, of course. I'll get eight, or sixteen, but . . ."

"Two each," Grijpstra said.

"Let Mr. Beelema go," de Gier said, "he understood."

Beelema returned. Zhaver had laid the table. Beelema joined his guests and observed them while they ate.

"I'm proud of you," Beelema said when they were done. "You didn't mess about. Where do we go from here?"

Grijpstra turned slowly. He observed the crowd at the bar. The South American low-cut lady admonished the mustachioed South American gentlemen. Two groups of glass-in-hand locals flanked the foreign element.

"Introduce me to somebody who knows the Fortunes, a reliable somebody. Can you do that?"

"Yes," Beelema said. He walked over to the locals and studied them one by one. He made his choice. "Mr. Hyme," Beelema whispered, "do you see the two men sitting at the corner table? They are police officers. They want to meet you. Please go and talk to them."

10

"Sir," Hyme said and contemplated the foam on his beer. "Sir, your question fascinates me. I asked myself the same question, last night, to be precise, when Beelema told me that Rea had gone and left an empty apartment. A most interesting question. Where is Rea Fortune? Or may we formulate it differently? *Is* Rea Fortune? The *where* could be immaterial, and if we should pursue that side, we might find ourselves in the Hereafter of parapsychology or the Bardo of Tibetan migrants. I believe that I understand the direction of your reasoning, and I agree in anticipation. Especially since I met with Fortune, just now in fact, on my way here. The man's mood is peculiar, victoriously nervous it seemed to me. And the tale he told me does not fit the past, if that past were decent, which we doubt, do we not? He told me that he is now eager to sell his business, while only a week ago the possibility drove him into a frenzy."

Grijpstra smiled cheerfully. Hyme smiled back. De Gier glanced out of the window. Hyme, dressed like a British sportsman of the early twenties and affecting the whiny tone of voice that is respectable in some provinces but antagonizes the denizens of the capital, irritated the sergeant. The view the window offered irritated him too. He had seen the elegant hairy cyclist before, he had heard the clanging pedal before. He forced himself to listen to Hyme and to neither kick nor hit Grijpstra. It was a pity that Grijpstra had so little intelligence, de Gier thought. He found a burned match in the ashtray, inserted it into his mouth, and began to chew slowly and rhythmically.

"Victoriously nervous," repeated Grijpstra, "exactly sir. The very impression the suspect made on me, when we interrogated him earlier today."

"As if he had succeeded in the undertaking of an important project," Hyme continued, "as if he had surmounted certain risks. Do you know what I thought when I reflected on our recent meeting?" ("No?" Grijpstra asked eagerly.) "I thought of the possibility that Frits Fortune is engaged in the Great Clearing. He rids himself of everything. First of all of his home, then of his work. Isn't that what life consists of? Home and work? Aren't both stress situations? Isn't home the worst of the two? Shouldn't home come first? If our lives contain too much hardness, if suffering out-balances pleasure, will we not destroy first the one and then the other?"

"*Right!*" Grijpstra shouted. "A type of suicide?" Grijpstra asked meekly.

"And reincarnation. But not in the hereafter, no, *here*. That was the impression Fortune gave me. Everything goes but he stays here. Remarkable, don't you think?"

Why does he wear a tie? the sergeant thought. That

man is an asshole. Why does he wear a blazer? Why
is he so happy? De Gier's thoughts colored the atmosphere, weighed it down, but Hyme pushed ahead.
Perhaps he noticed the threat, for he spoke both louder
and faster, and his hands, which had grabbed at Grijpstra's cigar smoke before, found a more useful occupa-
tion in producing a newspaper and folding it artfully
so that it became a triangular hat, of the type old-
fashioned children will wear.

"Yes, adjutant, the disappearance of Rea Fortune,
a charming woman engaged with the short end of the
stick throughout her short and unhappy life—she can't
have been older than thirty-five when I saw her last—"
("Yes?" Grijpstra asked compassionately) "is surrounded by doubt." Hyme focused his eyes triumphantly. "Doubt!"

De Gier's chewing changed. He abandoned the
earlier method of simple chomping and replaced it by
repetitive sucking and flattening.

Zhaver, at Grijpstra's request, brought more beer.

Hyme patted his paper headgear into shape and
placed it on the table. He stretched both arms and
nodded pleasantly.

"Doubt. And why do I doubt Rea's so-called volun-
tary retreat followed by a complete failure on Frits's
part to retrieve her presence? I doubt, for the one-
among-other-reasons that this very same Rea practically embraced me when I offered Frits Fortune, at
this same table a week ago, a cool million for his assorted rubbish, against my personal inclination, although the urgency of my associates' desire to take
over Frit's's business might have warranted such a
price." Hyme sighed briefly. "Did Frits accept? He did
not. Was he sorry? No, he was angry. Was he very
angry? He was furious. An emotion of that caliber is

not without its deeper meaning. It isn't necessary to have studied psychology, as I have . . ."

"Really?" Grijpstra asked admiringly.

". . . to conclude that Frits's personality began to split at that moment. A new personality attempted to emerge: new Frits trampled old Frits and confronted me, a once trusted friend."

Zhaver brought more beer, at Hyme's request.

Hyme collapsed. The beer supplied new energy. His voice dropped. His hand touched Grijpstra's knee. "We had been drinking, my guests and I. The stage was set well and I meant to give joy. Was I thanked? I was not. Frits stalked out of here; Rea followed sadly. What happened afterward? Can we surmise?" Hyme took his hand from Grijpstra's knee. "Was Rea a dragon, and did new Frits become a knight without fear?"

"Or blame," de Gier said.

"With blame," Hyme whispered.

De Gier stood up. His chair screeched on the boards. Hyme coughed, shielding his mouth politely. "Suicide and reincarnation, and the new birth financed by a million florins to ease the black knight's future path."

Grijpstra ordered a box of expensive cigars. Hyme accepted a cigar, reached again, and put a handful in his breast pocket.

De Gier combed his hair in the rest room. Except for the detectives and Hyme, there were no clients in the café.

Beelema returned from having walked Kiran in the street. "Titania hasn't come back yet?"

"Not yet," Zhaver said. "I shouldn't have joked about her predicament. True love is admirable. She has loved Fortune since he bought her those flowers."

De Gier came back. "Flowers?"

"Two dozen roses. Beelema and I forgot about

Titania's birthday although we remembered the year before, and Titania complained. She cried. Frits Fortune was here and a flower cart happened to pass. He rushed outside and bought the roses. A sentimental gesture and the undoing of Titania."

"Because Fortune is a serious man," Beelema said. "Titania isn't used to his type, she is used to the others."

"Fornicators," Zhaver said, "like us."

"Whom she tries to avoid."

"Not too successfully," Zhaver said.

"Which makes her feel worse," Beelema said.

Zhaver smiled. "Frits Fortune is a serious gentleman left by his wife, a handsome man still in the strength of his late youth and blessed with ample income. Titania is a lonely and beautiful woman looking for appreciation and solidity. If those two could meet, even for a moment, everlasting joy would surely result. I would like to see such bliss. True love, harmonious and lasting. It would encourage me. Why don't you arrange it, Borry? You claim divine parentage, it's your sort of thing."

Beelema nodded, shifted on his stool, bent his elbows on the counter, rested his head in his hands, and closed his eyes.

Grijpstra and de Gier studied Beelema.

Hyme said goodbye and left the café quietly.

Zhaver put his hands to his lips and moved to the far end of the bar. The detectives followed him.

"Sshh," Zhaver whispered, "he's thinking, it may take a while. What will be your pleasure?"

"Coffee," Grijpstra said, "for me and my sergeant." He smiled. "I was glad to meet Mr. Hyme. He argues along sensible lines and he is a reliable gent." He turned to de Gier. "I don't understand your negative attitude, Rinus. I'm going to telephone Cardozo and

Public Works. They'll have to produce a digger and be quick about it. Weekend work is healthy and pays double."

"Please, Grijpstra."

"I don't quite know what you're talking about," Zhaver said, "but Mr. Hyme is not a reliable gent."

"No?" Grijpstra asked. "No? A director of the best known publishing house of this country? A gentleman who dresses as a gentleman, who behaves as a gentleman?"

"Don't talk like the American lady in Paris," de Gier said. "A gentleman is a gentleman is a gentleman."

"Rose," Zhaver said. "Rose. Not gentleman. Do me a favor and please look out of that window, so that I can share my suffering. Throughout the week he holds himself together, but the weekends are too much, like now. Again and again. Isn't that type of behavior degenerate? Or am I old-fashioned? I think it is degenerate."

Hyme straddled the bridge railing in feeble but ecstatic balance. The triangular paper hat rested on his elongated skull. His penis rested on the tops of two fingers. A thick foaming jet of sunlit fluid raced to the sky before—gracefully forced by gravity—curving downward to unite with the passive and gleaming canal water.

"No," said Grijpstra.

"Yes," said de Gier. "As if you couldn't have known. Why did you have to force it? Forget your imagination and join the party. Nothing whatsoever is the matter. We are in a café in the inner city of Amsterdam. Life is bad but we can put up with it here. And when we're done, we'll go for a nice little walk and look at the geese if you like. A Hondecoeter theme, remember?" He clenched his fist and shook it in Grijpstra's face. "Cheer up. It's all right."

Beelema opened his eyes.

"It's not all right, but we can rectify the situation. Zhaver, it won't be easy but I can do it, as you say. Fetch Titania and tell her to wear her new jacket and skirt."

"With this heat?"

Beelema sighed. "You want me to do it or not? You want to obstruct or assist? Is it your fate or Titania's?"

"This is *it*," Grijpstra said. "This is *it* forever. I will no longer do this work. Everybody is quite abnormal in this town. I hereby grant them leave to destroy each other. I will, from now on, be sorting out traffic. No, because then I will still see them. I will be working in the clothing store at Headquarters. Not up front, but in the rear where nobody ever comes."

"I want to assist in achieving Titania's happiness," Zhaver said. "I'm sorry, Beelema."

"Go and fetch her then. She has to wear the long skirt, not that mini-rag. Her knees, first, will be covered or I won't even get into this. And a simple black blouse and something easy around her neck, that silk cord with the bone ring, she wore it the other day. She has to look neat."

"Neat," said Zhaver.

"Neat. And long silk stockings, no combination, real stockings, with real garters, she'll have some somewhere, and no panties."

Zhaver was at the door but stopped and turned.

"Is that neat?"

"Neat? What neat? What do I care about *neat?* We're concerned with Fortune's mind, and with contrast. What are you delaying the action for, Zhaver?"

"Right away, Borry."

"And I need her make-up kit, and a comb, and a brush."

They heard Zhaver crash up the stairs.

Beelema locked the front door. He closed the curtains and placed a chair in the middle of the room. He arranged the lights.

Titania came in and was directed to the chair. She sobbed pitifully.

"I can't help it that I fell in love. And that he never notices me. Never *wants* to notice me. Because I'm a street girl. Heeheehee."

"Don't cry, Titania."

"Heeheehee."

Beelema talked into her ear.

"This is your big day, Titania. The prince is coming."

"What prince, heeheehee?"

"Prince Frits the First. He loves you but he doesn't know that yet, because he doesn't know your true shape. We're going to work on your true shape. You're not what you think you are. You are a princess."

"Yes?"

"Yes. Easy now, Titania. You're an easy princess. Lovable on a high level, as I'm about to indicate. Here, a little here, and a little here too, close your eyes or I'll glue your lashes together, this shit is sticky, and a little there, oops, rub it away a mite. Aren't you incredible now? And you'll have a small accident, and the prince will be there to save you and take you to his castle. It's a bit empty his castle, but never mind, there'll be a mattress I hear, and that's all you need. A round of fahdee-foozle, a shower together, a bowl of soup and a sandwich shared in the main chamber, or in the royal kitchen maybe, and your souls will be linked. You'll never work again, Titania. We'll miss you maybe but nobody is irreplaceable, we'll find another so that the clients can have a fresh view, two fresh views, haha. Don't pull faces, Titania, or I can't do your mouth."

Borry Beelema worked on and continued his monologue. He rubbed color on her cheekbones and wiped most of it away again. He stood back.

"You'll have to be tragic, Titania, and decent, but sensual." He bowed down, adjusting lipstick. "Sit still, I've got to concentrate, or we get nowhere."

"Morons," Grijpstra said, "and not an exception among them. If they're in Amsterdam, they're morons. Sometimes I think I see a normal person, but the fault is mine. I've let myself be persuaded by weakness, by unhealthy idealism, but it won't happen again."

"I'm a little nauseous," de Gier said. "Maybe it's the matches. Don't you have any gum, Zhaver? Who would ever have thought that I would chew gum? And to think that I stopped Seeny on the corridor the other day and bothered her, and now I do it too."

"Here you are," Zhaver said. "This is supposed to taste like sour apples. Who is Seeny?"

"A constable from the radio room," Grijpstra said, "a well-shaped girl, but since he grabbed her by the throat and broke her jaws open and removed the gum from behind her back teeth, she doesn't like him anymore."

"Quiet!" said Beelema. "I've done it, Titania. From here we can proceed. The beginning is easy enough, you'll go outside, and so do we, to take care of you, for you're too lovely to be on your own now. All sorts of types are about and they all have loose hands, my work is not to be spoiled. We'll be with you, although we won't be in sight, and Zhaver will phone Frits. He does have a telephone, I hope, or did she take that too?"

"There was a phone on the wall," de Gier said.

"Splendid, that's all we need. Zhaver phones and says that he has, what do we have? Knockwurst? That he has some nice knockwurst for him, that we're about to close but that he can come in for a moment. He is home, see?" Beelema lifted a curtain. "The light is on." He dropped the curtain. "Frits comes here, and Zhaver feeds him the sausage. Then Zhaver says it's been a long day. Frits leaves again. And then you cross his path, Titania, and have your accident."

The girl smiled.

"Right away?"

Beelema arranged a hair that had jumped free of his careful arrangement.

"No, no, no. No hurry, please. First there'll be some conversation. He never saw you in this outfit, he won't even recognize you. I've changed and exaggerated, your eyes are bigger and your ears are all out. So you say, 'Hello, Frits,' softly and nicely, polite-like, but a little more. Say it, Titania."

"Hello, Frits."

"Okay. That'll stop him but that's not enough. He's got to be *with* you, so you touch his arm. Let's see, I'm Frits, I pass you; say it . . ."

"Hello, Frits."

"Perfect, hold my arm now, see? He's stuck, never to free himself again. And now, a few steps ahead, there's this brick sticking up, and you stumble and fall. Pay attention now, Titania, this is where it goes, you've got to grab him with sex, it's your only weapon in the end. He's got to think of the actual insertion, he's got to really want the ultimate contact. Do you get me?"

"Can't we kiss? I like kissing too."

"Yes, sure. It'll be a start, you can do that too, I don't mind. So you fall *and pull up your dress,* all the way up, he looks right into you, *but only for a moment,* for then it's gone. You pull your dress down again, if you stay there in your full glory, you overdo it, it'll be the end of it. Get me? Let's try. Move up, gentlemen, take your stools. Sit up straight, your heads will have to be on the same level as if you were standing. You're the committee. All set?"

"We're the committee," Grijpstra said.

Titania stumbled and fell. Dress up, dress down.

"No," Grijpstra said. "I didn't see anything. Too fast."

Beelema agreed. "We'll try again."

Later.

"Are you crazy?" Titania said. "I won't fall all night. And I'm not on show for nothing, certainly not underneath. Have you all gone out of your minds?" She took a deep breath.

"Don't say it!" Beelema had raised his arms. "That's it. You're in the right frame of mind now. Let's go."

11

It was Saturday night and the lush heat of summer hung under a clear and starry sky. Two red-beaked geese floated in the Emperorscanal and had almost reached the bridge at the edge of the Brewerscanal. The herring-stall on the bridge had closed.

Grijpstra and de Gier stood next to the stall and peered cautiously around it. Kiran sniffed at a tree. Beelema and Zhaver were present but invisible. A couple, arm in arm, approached slowly. The woman, clearly visible in the light of the bridge's lampposts, emitted a serene beauty from every particle of her body and clothing. She talked to the man in a low voice. She stumbled and fell. Frits Fortune reacted in fear and concern, he bent down, his arms reached. Titania groaned. Her skirt, made of pure and delicate wool and matching her long and elegant jacket, slipped up, ignor-ing the limits of decency.

A gentleman, in a three-piece summer suit and wearing an old-fashioned expensive felt hat, cycled toward the bridge. One of the pedals of his cycle clanged against the metal chain guard. The geese appeared at the other side of the bridge and greeted their new view, honking softly. Titania corrected her unruly skirt. Frits Fortune, with diminishing fear and growing concern, lifted the fallen woman and remembered how, in clear and almost touchable detail, the lady's thighs were soft and pink, and how they held and would still hold a promise of curly down that in turn protected a moist NO, he would think no further. He asked if she had hurt herself. She said she had, poor Titania.

On her feet, she leaned into his arms. The geese honked loudly, the cyclist was close. Beelema and Zhaver stepped back into the shadows between a pickup and a van, Grijpstra and de Gier held on to each other. Titania's lips pursed, opened slightly, her long lashes partly hid her soft and inviting eyes. Frits's mouth drew close to Titania's, the cyclist braked, the cycle fell, the object the cyclist pointed was made of blue steel.

"HO!" Grijpstra shouted.

De Gier was running, no, leaping. The cyclist flew sideward, propelled by the sudden contact with the sergeant's last and far-ranging leap. The shot rang out. The bullet whistled and splashed. The red-beaked geese flapped and blew in anger. The cyclist's hat dropped, and his wig, beard, and mustache moved to the side of her face.

Titania, suddenly released by Frits Fortune, staggered, stumbled, and fell. Her skirt, much higher now, translated the indicated into the obvious until once more corrected, as Titania, unaided, struggled up. Beelema and Zhaver came forward. Kiran waved his long tail. Fortune, Titania, Zhaver, and Beelema stared at the cyclist.

"Hello, Rea," Fortune said.

"Mrs. Fortune," Grijpstra said politely, "I arrest you, under suspicion of repeated attempted murder or manslaughter, as the case may be, of your husband, and of ill treatment of your dog Babette resulting in its death."

De Gier bent his knees and looked into Beelema's eyes.

"Are you the other son of God?"

"It was well meant," Beelema whispered hoarsely.

"It usually is," de Gier said.

"Are you coming with me?" Grijpstra asked Rea Fortune imperatively.

"Coming with me?" de Gier asked Beelema pleasantly.

"Coming?" Fortune asked Titania shyly.

Kiran embraced Zhaver, barking cheerfully.

12

"Well, well," the commissaris said, "and in the weekend too, in the off weekend! Will I ever understand what motivates activity? I do hope your reports will be short and limit the prosecutor's ridicule. A merry display indeed! Will you be holding Rea Fortune, adjutant?"

"I might recommend that to the authorities, sir," Grijpstra said. "I've charged the suspect with the illegal possession of a firearm."

"And the attempted manslaughter, albeit murder?"

"We might drop that part of the charge, sir. The suspect is in a state of shock, the material we've come up with is somewhat garbled, and the lawyer the suspect hired seems to be rather forceful, and, eh, intelligent, sir. It seems that Mrs. Fortune was merely persuading her husband to sell his business, by manipulating circumstances, so to speak. I gather that she thought that the sudden emptiness of their apartment, coupled with her own and the dog's disappearance, would make him change his mind. By weakening his defenses by, as the lawyer puts it, not illegal means, she meant to release the victim of his fear of retirement."

The commissaris harrumphed furiously.

"And the evidence you found? Fortune's weak heart? His susceptibility to sudden shocks? The actual death of that poor little poodle? Can't we show a sinister underground? And what about Beelema, the divine entrepreneur, surely he can be charged with complicity?"

"The evidence could be rather thin, sir."

"And the count? That Zhaver fellow? He was her lover, wasn't he?"

"So was Beelema, sir, but the two of them stood to gain nothing. They weren't being paid and there was no promise of payment. Neither of them meant to marry Mrs. Fortune or live with her. The relationship was merely physical, it seems."

"So what were they? Friends? Did they help the lady to move the contents of the apartment?"

"No sir."

"Who *did* help her?"

"Illegal immigrants, sir, Turks and Pakistanis. There are quite a few of them in the neighborhood. They're always looking for jobs."

"Are you sure?"

"I have no reason to disbelieve the suspect, sir, but the sergeant and I can check the point if you like."

The commissaris whipped off his spectacles and began to polish them with his handkerchief.

"Ha! No. I won't go against your judgment. You might explain, however, why the lady did dress up as a man and cycle around in the area."

"To see how her husband was doing."

"Ah. And the dog?"

"Rea lived in a hotel, sir. The dog was confused. It got away from her and ran home. She picked it up the next day; she still had the key, of course, but it was still nervous, crossed the street and was killed by a car."

The commissaris blew on his glasses.

"Hold it there, adjutant, how did the body get on the roof?"

Grijpstra scratched his chin.

"She put it there, didn't she?" the commissaris asked. "Now why would she do that? She could have dropped it in a garbage can, but she went to a lot of trouble to hide it in an unlikely place. Would she be hoping perhaps that Fortune, who was still doing well and not suffering enough perhaps, might be disturbed by the gulls and crows, climb onto the roof, and find the torn corpse of a pet he was fond of? Another shock to shake the poor fellow's mind perhaps?"

Grijpstra scratched his chin with a little more force.

"Could be, sir."

The commissaris frowned.

"Bad, adjutant, bad. To misuse affection. She had done it before, after all, by running away, thinking that Frits would miss her. Consistent behavior. Do you think the woman is evil?"

Grijpstra sighed.

The commissaris replaced his spectacles and managed to smile.

"Bah. But you're right not to pursue the point. Her lawyer would tell the court that the means justify the end somewhat, and the end was to help. Wives are supposed to help their husbands. They rarely do. And the means never justify the end, but that's between you and me. The lawyer will also mention that the dog was already dead. So what does all this add up to?"

Grijpstra grunted. The commissaris got up, left his desk, and found the center of his carpet.

"Now what caused you two to waste two free days on such a flimsy case, eh? And why didn't you spot the suspect? Isn't it hard for a woman to impersonate a man? If I understand the situation correctly, she must have shown herself to you on several occasions."

The Oriental arrows extended from his shoes. One arrow pointed at Grijpstra, the other at de Gier.

De Gier plotted the course of the arrow. When he realized the danger, he spoke.

"The suspect used to be an actress, sir, possibly a good actress. I believe she was a professional. I saw her too and I never caught on. I only noticed that the cyclist was slender, well dressed, and overhairy. I've seen worse in the city, perhaps my mind no longer registers abnormalities. All sorts of apparitions appear these days. There was a dwarf, for instance, dressed in a yellow cape. He rode a scooter, a monkey sat on the handlebars."

The commissaris's mouth opened as he tried to visualize the yellow-caped dwarf.

"Really? What sort of a scooter, a motor scooter?"

"No sir, a child's scooter."

"And he wasn't a child?"

"No sir, he had a beard too, and a mustache."

"For heaven's sake."

Grijpstra gestured. "Amsterdam, sir!"

Grijpstra offered a cigar. The commissaris was calmed by the sudden intake of nicotine.

"Dwarf! Well. Ah. Something else. The lady pulled a gun. She actually fired the gun. Did she aim at the kissing couple?"

"She didn't have time, sir, the sergeant knocked her off her feet."

"But the shot went off so she had pressed the safety catch. Did you question her on that point?"

"Yes sir, she said that she intended to fire over their heads. She confesses to being jealous but there was no murderous intent."

"Is she a good shot?"

"No sir, she had never fired a gun, except on the stage where they use blanks."

The commissaris sucked his cigar.

"Yes. Hmpf. So she could have shot them by mistake or she could have got someone else, so perhaps it was a good thing you two were around, to prevent an accident. You know . . ."

A streetcar passed down the Marnixstreet outside and the commissaris had to wait for the noise to subside.

"You two remind me of a farewell speech delivered by my first chief who retired. That was a long time ago, but truth lasts. I wore a saber on my belt then, and performed street duty."

"What did your chief say, sir?"

"You really want to know? Very well. He claimed that the police are by definition stupid, because intelligent men will not apply for boring work at low wages. He also said that stupidity hardly matters in our profession, provided our brainlessness is compensated by zeal."

"Zeal . . . ," Grijpstra muttered.

"Weren't you and the sergeant zealous, by working when you didn't have to?"

De Gier got up.

"Could I bother you for a match, sir?"

The commissaris flicked his golden lighter.

"No, a match. To chew on, sir."

"Chew? Oh, I see. You're still not smoking. No, I don't have a match, sergeant. Grijpstra?"

The adjutant passed a box of matches. De Gier began to chew hungrily. Grijpstra moved his chair. The arrow no longer pointed at his feet. The commissaris stepped off the carpet and yanked a corner. The arrow followed Grijpstra. The commissaris stepped back.

"Perhaps the chief's statement was too abstract, but

he accompanied it with a story. Would you like to hear the story too?"

"Yes," de Gier said.

"You too, adjutant?"

"Yes."

"Good, because I would have told it anyway. Listen here."

Grijpstra moaned.

"Adjutant?"

"I *did* have serious suspicions, sir. The sergeant is smiling, and it's true that he hasn't gone along with me much, but I refuse to believe that my theory was silly. Rea Fortune did disappear with her dog and the contents of the house. An exceptional course of events has often provided me with a case. We found nothing but dust specks in that apartment. Unusual, sir, very."

"Yes?"

"There were character witnesses," Grijpstra said sadly. "Several, in fact. They confirmed the suspect's tendency, I'm referring to *Mr.* Fortune now, to destroy what he didn't like. Isn't a character the sum of certain habits, and aren't habits with us forever?"

"I used to smoke," de Gier said, "but I don't anymore."

"Arrgh!"

"Just thought I would mention it."

"Not again!"

"So a man is a slave," de Gier said, "the slave of what he did. For what he did, you say, he does, and what he does, you say, he will always do. There's also liberty, I just thought I would mention liberty."

The commissaris left his carpet and studied a geranium.

Grijpstra glared.

De Gier smiled. "I *did* stop smoking, you know. I chew matches now, different habit altogether."

"We know, we know," the commissaris said to the geranium. "He stopped smoking. Now why would he have done that?"

"For Grijpstra, sir."

Grijpstra jumped up.

"Won't you ever stop saying that? What is it to me whether you smoke or not?"

De Gier moved his match with his tongue.

"To show you that there is still hope."

"Hope. For who?"

"For you."

"Not for me. I'm stuck. I waste my time watching morons because anything is better than to stay home. A situation that can't be changed."

"If I can change, so can you. To smoke is to be addicted. I broke my chain. I'm free." De Gier got up and clutched his belt. "Would you excuse me a minute? Chewing matches doesn't agree with me. I'll be right back."

He looked pale when he came back and there was a sour stench.

"Won't you go back to smoking again?" the commissaris asked.

"Not just yet, sir."

"Then I'll tell you the story to distract you. *A jack rabbit runs through a field. He doesn't pay attention. He runs into a fence. The impact stuns him for a moment. He staggers about for a bit. A few cows are around. The jack rabbit bumps into a cow. The second mishap is too much for him. The jack rabbit faints. He's under the cow. 'Look,' the cow says to the other cows, 'I actually managed to catch a jack rabbit.'* "

"That's about the way it was," de Gier said.

"Do you agree, adjutant?"

"Yes sir."

"I'm glad to hear it and I'm glad you were good

enough to keep me informed of your activities. You know that I don't have much of a function here, as the journalist of the *Courier* was kind enough to point out."

More streetcars passed through the Marnixstreet. The commissaris spent another minute on his geranium.

"And what do you think of our lovers, Grijpstra, do you think that the affair will last?"

"Frits Fortune and Titania?"

"Yes."

"I think so, sir. Titania is a dear girl and I was mistaken about Mr. Fortune, I believe he's a good man. She certainly managed to impress him at the right moment."

"In which case you'll have to find a suitable partner for Rea, we cannot let go of her now. She'll be depressed and slip into even worse ideas. Perhaps Beelema should exercise his powers again, keeping the lady's extravagant desires in mind. How about matching her to the nobleman Xavier Michel d'Ablaing de Batagglia? The capital which will be returned to her by Frits Fortune could ease her way with him. Zhaver has gone straight for a long while; perhaps the two of them could start up a luxurious restaurant."

"Yes sir."

The commissaris rubbed his legs. His lips thinned.

"A change of weather, gentlemen, I feel it in my bones. Perhaps we should do some real work for a change. I had a call just before you came in. A well-dressed male corpse was found in the luggage compartment of a stolen Mercedes." He tore a sheet out of his notebook and gave it to Grijpstra. The sergeant read the notes over the adjutant's shoulder.

"A corpse!" de Gier said. "Just what is needed."

When the detectives crossed the hall on their way to the elevator, Grijpstra held on to de Gier's arm.

"Didn't you mention a dwarf in a yellow cape on a scooter just now?"

"I don't smoke anymore," de Gier said.

"With a monkey on the handlebars?"

"A withdrawal monkey," de Gier said, "and a withdrawal dwarf."

"Is that what you see? But that's horrifying. I'll never stop smoking."

"What has that got to do with it?" de Gier asked. "Smoking is fun."

"So you'll start again?"

"Me? No. I don't smoke. Not smoking is becoming a habit and habits are forever."

De Gier walked on. Grijpstra walked after him. De Gier frowned. Grijpstra grinned.

PART II

1

De Gier crossed the courtyard. His legs bounced, his arms swung, his chin jutted, the sun highlighted his wavy hair. Grijpstra followed heavily, as if the tarmac stuck to his soles, as if the air was viscous, as if his blood was glue, coagulating in every artery and vein. De Gier folded himself into the Volkswagen and waited, drumming his fingertips on the steering wheel. He started the engine as Grijpstra lowered his bulk on the creaking plastic next to him. Grijpstra mumbled.

The car left the courtyard and headed for the inner city, ignoring traffic signals, swerving around jaywalking pedestrians.

"I don't know what you're saying," de Gier said, "but here's your corpse. You looked for it all weekend. You were right, after all; whatever you want will find you in due time." He patted Grijpstra's shoulder. "A solid corpse, adjutant, all ours. No manufactured case this time. We won't have to make excuses to each other and to the good citizens who obstruct our path. We can work by the book. We're following orders. Forward."

"Forward how?" Grijpstra asked and nodded at a gesticulating oversized lady on a bicycle as the car eased through a red light.

"From dream time into actuality," de Gier shouted as he made the Volkswagen shoot ahead. "A real body, quite dead but able to withstand our prodding. Facts instead of a vacuum. Cause and effect instead of conjecture on a transparent tightrope. Connecting events instead of stacking flimsy cards!"

Grijpstra mumbled on.

De Gier parked.

"We can walk from here. We even have an address. Gentleman's Market. Across the canal, see? There's the Mercedes, there's a patrol car. We have all sorts of details. A silver Mercedes with a German registration. Corpse of a forty-five-year-old man, well dressed. Isn't it unbelievable, Grijpstra, after all we've been through?"

Grijpstra grunted, spoke, and grunted again.

"What's that?"

"I'm saying," Grijpstra said in an unnecessarily loud voice, "that we are back where we started, on the Brewerscanal, with nothing in our hands. Once again we will twist misrepresented evidence and be a bother to ourselves and all those who have the misfortune to meet with us. What do we have?" He held up a finger. "A corpse, you're right. From that point on, you're wrong. The corpse was not killed, neither by itself nor by others. There are, according to the commissaris's notes, no wounds. Very likely our man died of natural causes. If we get into this, we'll stumble forever, and there'll be nothing in the end."

De Gier got out of the car, walked around it and

opened the passenger door. He reached in, grabbed Grijpstra by the forearm and pulled.

"No. I'm right. We have a case. The corpse was found in the baggage compartment of a car. How did it get there?"

They crossed the nearest bridge. A male and a female constable walked toward the detectives.

"I'll tell you how it got there," Grijpstra said. "It fell in. It was still alive then. The man became unwell, the baggage compartment of the car was open, he lunged toward the car, intending to find support, he was dizzy, fainting, he tumbled into the gaping hole."

"And somebody closed the lid," de Gier said. "No, no. Murder. I tell you it's murder. We're employed by the murder brigade. This is our thing. The hunt is on. Hello, Asta, hello, Karate, where's Ketchup?"

"Do you know my name?" Asta asked.

"Ketchup is on leave," Karate said. "The weekend was too much for him. He scraped some free days together and foul-mouthed Sergeant Jurriaans. The sergeant jumped across the counter, but Ketchup was out on the street by then. He's a good runner. Look what I got in his place."

"I'm not a what," Asta said. "I'm a she. I have my rights. I didn't know you knew my name, sergeant."

"Stay away from him," Grijpstra said. "He's working, but not for long. This corpse is nothing, we'll find something else to do. We could have a late breakfast or an early lunch. Where's the dead man, constable?"

Asta stopped smiling at de Gier. "Taken away, adjutant, there were too many people around, it was causing an obstruction. It has been photographed, and the doctor was here. The ambulance took it to the morgue. The doctor thought the man may have died of natural causes. He suspected a stomach ulcer that broke and caused a bleeding."

"See?" Grijpstra asked. *"See!"* Grijpstra shouted. "Isn't that what I said just now? Let's go, sergeant. We'll visit the morgue, meet with the doctor, and have a meal. I won't waste one unnecessary minute on this routine accident."

"Let's see the car," de Gier said.

"The lid of the baggage compartment was closed," Karate said, "but not quite. The lock had been forced, you see. We have the car on the stolen list, it disappeared sometime during the night. It had been parked in front of Hotel Oberon. The owner of the car stays there. I met him this morning before we went out on patrol. A fat German, wheezing and bubbling. He told us the car cost a lot of money and that we had to drop everything and look for it."

De Gier turned to Asta. "Were you there too?"

"Yes," Asta said, "he was the same man who wouldn't pay his bill at Beelema's. Didn't we do that little job well, sergeant? There can't have been more than two minutes between your telephone call and our arrival. Wasn't it great?"

"No," Grijpstra said.

"What was wrong with the way we handled that incident, adjutant?" Asta asked.

"What? Oh, nothing. You're paid to do your job well, aren't you? I don't want this case, sergeant. It's the same thing again. I got away from it and now we're back. Beelema, I don't want to hear that name again. And that German was obnoxious, he'll still be obnoxious. I'm glad his car was stolen." He hit the trunk with his flat hand. "Is this the only damage, constable? Just a broken lock?"

"Yes."

"Pity. Thieves took the car and forced the baggage compartment. They left, either finding nothing or taking what they found. The car remained. Our fellow staggers along and falls into it. He dies."

"Who closed the lid?"

Grijpstra shrugged.

"Who cares? Some person who passed the car and didn't like the gaping rear end. He pulled the lid down without looking at the possible contents of the baggage compartment. He saw something that shouldn't be and corrected the situation. I'm like that too. Last night, on my way home, I saw the wheel of a bicycle lying in the street. Shouldn't be there, might cause an accident. I picked it up and left it with some garbage cans so that it could be picked up this morning by the collectors. There are many people like me. A passer-by who closed the lid. It was dark, the streetlights are at some distance. Did the lock work when the lid was closed?"

"It held," Karate said, "but it had been tampered with."

"How did the car get here? Did the thieves have a key?"

"No, they hot-wired the engine."

"How did you find the corpse?"

Karate took off his cap and scratched his head.

"Well?"

"I don't want to upset you, adjutant."

De Gier pushed Grijpstra gently aside. "Tell me, Karate. I'm all right this morning. It's a beautiful day. This is a nice case. I'm glad we're working together again. Tell me all you know, Karate."

Karate replaced his cap. "Very well, sergeant. Mrs. Cabbage-Tonto checked in with us this morning. She has a small dog, very small, a Chihuahua, I believe it's called. Looks like the wrong sort of mouse. The dog had to pee, she was taking it for a walk on a leash. The dog pulled her to the Mercedes, peed for a bit and started yelling or squeaking. That kind of dog doesn't bark, I

believe. She dragged it away and it went on peeing and
it did the other thing too, maybe it even threw up, it
was in a proper state, sergeant. It wanted to get back to
the car and had another fit. Mrs. Cabbage-Tonto, she
claimed to know the adjutant—Sergeant Jurriaans didn't
want to listen to her at first—said that she knew somebody really high up in the force and would complain,
and she described the adjutant, fat man in a pinstripe
suit and big cheeks, she said, so we knew it was Adjutant Grijpstra . . ."

"Ho!" Grijpstra said.

"Yes?" Karate asked.

"Never mind."

"Right," Karate said. "So Mrs. Cabbage-Tonto said
she found the dead man. She looked into the baggage
compartment. The lock closed but didn't lock, if you
see what I mean, because it had been forced. The witness ran all the way to the station, dragging the dog. It
had sore paws when it arrived and sort of cried. It had
to stand in a tray filled with water for a while to cool
its feet."

"Go on."

"The lady didn't strike us as a reliable witness, but
as she knew the adjutant and our station has had trouble with the adjutant before, Sergeant Jurriaans thought
we might have a look. We found the corpse all right. It
looked peaceful, folded into itself, but it was covered
with blood."

"Could you ascertain its identity?"

"Yes, sergeant. The doctor gave us the wallet he
found in its jacket. The man is called Jim Boronski."

"A foreigner," Grijpstra said, "we don't want that, a
foreign corpse isn't easy to deal with."

Karate smiled helpfully. "He was Dutch, adjutant.
The wallet contained a passport. Born in Rotterdam,

now residing in Colombia, South America. A business-man. He also carried a hotel key, from Hotel Oberon."

Grijpstra groaned.

"Beautiful," de Gier said. "As I thought. We can link facts already. So our man drops dead into the car of a fellow hotel guest. Continue, constable."

Karate spread his small hands. "That's about it, ser-geant. The corpse was dressed in a well-made suit of good material. Apart from the blood, it looked well-cared for. I don't recall seeing the man in this district."

Grijpstra crossed the quay, studied the green water of the canal for a while, and came back. "Very well, we'll look into this. When did you find the corpse?"

Karate produced his notebook and flipped the pages. "Here, adjutant, 10:04 this morning. The doctor took it away at 10:30, it's 12:30 now, we waited for you."

Grijpstra scribbled in his notebook. De Gier looked at Asta. He remembered Sergeant Jurriaans's tale re-layed by Grijpstra. He tried to visualize her as she must have been during that adventurous night but could only see a neatly dressed constable with inordinately sparkly eyes, now smiling politely. "I wish I were a detective," she was saying. "This job is boring, bah, smelly."

De Gier peeked at the bloodstained baggage com-partment of the Mercedes. "Smelly? But this is fresh."

Asta peeked too. "The corpse was fine. I meant the chicken remains earlier on. Another complaint we took care of this morning. There's a Chinese in that sidestreet over there who slaughters poultry and dumps the left-overs in the street. The garbage collectors won't pick it up and the stuff rots. The Chinese won't bag it for he says bags are too expensive. Or so he seems to say. I don't speak Chinese."

"Yes," de Gier said.

The girl stood closer. "What will you do now, sergeant? Is this a murder? Is there a killer around? Will you find him?"

"Maybe."

"You will, won't you? I hear you always find the killer."

De Gier returned her smile. "Your informants exaggerated." He looked at Grijpstra. "We've been known to fail." He touched his breast, then patted his other pockets.

The girl took a packet of cigarettes from her bag. "Would you like one?"

"No thank you. I don't smoke."

They had to step aside. Municipal workers were trying to park some road machinery and a sooty tank on wheels approached dangerously. An unmuffled engine started up and heavy drills bit into the tarmac.

Grijpstra shouted into de Gier's ear. "Let's go to the morgue and raise Cardozo. If there's any work he can do it."

De Gier shouted back. "Cardozo is sick, didn't you see the note on your desk just now?"

Grijpstra walked to the car, but had to come back to release de Gier from Asta's smile. He pushed the sergeant into a slow walk. "How sick is Cardozo?"

"Flu, may take a few days."

"Useless fellow. Who'll do the routine? That Boronski has no address here, he probably doesn't even have relatives in the city. If he had he wouldn't be staying in a hotel. We'll have to circulate his photograph, see what we can find out about him. We may have some time-consuming sleuthing to do."

"Yes," de Gier said, "but there's no hope of help in the brigade; it's holiday time and we're short-staffed."

"Get help."

"Yes, adjutant. Do you care where I get it?"

"No."

"Wait for me in the car."

Grijpstra smiled as he saw de Gier walk into a to-bacconist's store. It took a while before the sergeant came back, but he wasn't smoking.

"What did you do in there?"

"I phoned, of course. I spoke with Sergeant Jur-riaans. We have help. He's lending us Asta. He will order her to go home and change into civilian clothes. We are to pick her up later; I have the address."

Grijpstra snorted. *"You* pick her up. You're an idiot, Rinus, I warned you. That girl can't be more than twenty-five years old and Jurriaans is my age, in his fifties. She isn't right in the head, neither are you at this particular time. You sure you didn't buy cigarettes in that store?"

"Yes. To the morgue?"

"To the morgue," Grijpstra said cheerfully and grinned at his thoughts. They were in color and three-dimensional. His jealousy evaporated as he contem-plated his vision. The central part of it was Asta with-out any clothes on, kneeling, her left hand held by Grijpstra who was dressed in a long silk robe. His free hand blessed the girl, who, with downcast eyes, de-murely accepted the benediction. Her right hand was stretched out in the direction of a reclining naked male body, peacefully asleep on a well-kept lawn. The body carried a noble face with a full mustache and shiny curly hair.

I'm giving her to him, Grijpstra thought, as he took in more details of the vision. The little group was sur-rounded by orange trees close to a pond where interest-ing hard-to-define animals cavorted in pure water. The sky was cloudy, but had opened to frame a mysterious faraway figure shrouded in light. That must be God, Grijpstra thought. That's good, that makes me an angel.

I don't want to be God, but to be an angel must be all right. They get to do things.

Like giving away, he thought a little later as the Volkswagen found a place in the small courtyard next to the city's morgue, a low building built out of glowing red bricks that belied the cold finality of its contents. It's better to give than to receive. Besides, he thought as he wrung himself out of the compact, I don't want to be hassled by females, no matter how superior they may be. De Gier still likes it. All I want is . . .

Not quite knowing what he wanted, he didn't finish the thought.

2

"Gentlemen," the small man said, "your client is waiting for you. He hasn't been in storage for more than five minutes. The doctor is done with him and is now washing his hands."

He restrained Grijpstra who was about to light a cigar. Grijpstra frowned.

The attendant raised his hands in helpless defense.

"Regulations, adjutant. They still apply to the living. The dead are free, they may do as they like in peace. You're welcome to smoke in my office." He opened a door and pointed at a table where a collection of pipes surrounded a full ashtray.

De Gier looked at the neatly labeled drawers of the massive refrigerator in the back of the room.

"Boronski. Here we are." He pulled. The drawer came faster than he expected and the corpse's face, slightly twisted to the side, looked up at him with an expression of furious surrender.

"Easy," Grijpstra said and put an arm around the sergeant's shoulders. "You should remember that nicotine no longer dulls your fears." He swiveled the sergeant's body and walked him away from the extended drawer.

"Can't stand it, can he?" the attendant asked. "I don't blame him. Took me a while to get used to them too, and I've lived with them for a long time. But they're not here, of course. A few will linger for a while. I can feel that, but I talk to them, polite-like, and they go away. There's nothing here for them and most should have better places to go to. I tell them that I'm just a crazy guy who works here, that I mean no harm. They're frightened, you know, whatever they were used to is no longer there. Alive yesterday, dead today, must be a bit of a change."

De Gier's nausea slipped away as he listened to the attendant's quiet voice. The man's beady eyes behind round little glasses seemed unfocused, his trousers were so short that they showed white skin above the crumpled socks, his green coat was partly unbuttoned. He wore a skull cap.

"Jacobs is the name," the small man said. "You won't remember me, sergeant, but I've seen you here before. Don't feel shy about showing your weakness. There's something wrong with the man who has to show his self-control at all times. If you want to know what your corpse died of you better see the doctor before he gets away."

They were ushered into another room where the doctor was looking at his notebook, circling words with a pencil.

"You're here for Boronski? Interesting case in a way, and so is the other, the one your colleagues brought in yesterday. Have a look at her before you leave. Attractive young gal, also found in the trunk of a car. Had been there a while, but not long enough for the heroin traces to disappear. The white stuff in the corners of her mouth are maggot eggs, by the way. I thought it was spittle at first, but it wasn't. Maggots breed fast in this kind of hot weather."

"Murdered?" Grijpstra asked.

The doctor laughed. "No, no, that's all you chaps think about. Murder. Manslaughter. Violence. Most people die by accident, you know, out of stupidity. I believe there was a party in a villa somewhere; young people amusing themselves. This gal took an overdose, heroin has to be measured carefully, but she was a young girl, there were people about, dancing, making love. She didn't pay attention, injected herself in a hurry and croaked. Nobody noticed her death for a while, then they found her. Nobody knew who she was either. She was picked up, taken to the party, and there she was, dead. They meant to dump her, put her in a car, and forgot all about the matter. Body started to smell after a few days, the car was parked in the sun. Somebody noticed and stopped a patrol car. The owner of the car was found, and he said he didn't know at first. Later he remembered, vaguely. It all checked out. Your colleagues were upset because they didn't have a case, not even death through negligence. The girl is over twenty-one, she injected herself, she was put in the car without the owner's proper consent, he didn't know what was asked of him, being stoned himself. And then he forgot. Drove her around for days in his brand new supercar. Pleasant young fellow apparently. Bit of an addict. Won't live long himself. Well, gentlemen, what can I do for you?"

"Boronski, sir," Grijpstra said.

"Boronski. What can I tell you? He died around midnight. My original diagnosis was confirmed by the subsequent tests. Man was suffering of a really bad duodenal ulcer, enormous. Must have formed quickly, came to a head, the stomach perforated, and the flow of blood and pus upset his insides. He sort of choked internally. Severe cramps, must have doubled up, literally vomited his guts out and collapsed, I imagine. An extreme case indeed. He might have been saved if he had been taken to hospital immediately. Still a fairly young fellow too and no trace of other ulcers, his first and his last. You chaps know anything about ulcers?"

"No," Grijpstra said.

"Really? Had one myself once, long time ago now. I'm only a corpse cutter, but I'm not altogether out of touch with what the other branches of the profession come up with. Ulcers are psychosomatic, they say. You know what that means?"

"Caused by a malfunctioning of the mind, sir?" de Gier asked.

"Yes. Emotional malfunction. The mind is emotional, so is the rest of the body. I'd have to find the book again, but I think I remember that ulcers, particularly duodenal ulcers, are caused by a sudden loss of faith, in another person or maybe in an idea, a comforting idea that falls away and is no longer comforting. Some frightening insight, caused by something not being there that should be there. Would be true in my case. I thought I had a wife and I didn't; she was still around at that time but not in the way I thought that she should be. She had a lover." He chuckled. "I was young then and thought I had rights. Nobody has rights. We've got what's coming to us. However, I, in my innocence, or ignorance, that's a better word, ignorance, insisted on things to be otherwise than they were. So I was punished by an ulcer. A little one, but it hurt, and I had to eat porridge for a while, yak, porridge, and pudding. The puddings weren't so bad. My wife made them and put cherries on top. Very nice of her. Then she left me altogether. There was another female for a while who comforted me and the ulcer healed. Hasn't bothered me again."

"About Boronski, sir."

"Yes?"

"Any bruises on the body?"

"No. The hands are scratched; he must have toppled over and scratched them on the cobblestones. I found traces of street dirt; it'll be in my report."

"But he wasn't found on the street, he was in the baggage compartment of a car."

The doctor dropped his notebook into his briefcase. The tiny lock of the case snapped in place.

"Really? Now how did he get there? Well, I've done my job, good luck to you. Have a look at that girl before you leave. Just out of interest. Maggot eggs, amazing."

The doctor left and the attendant came in and presented Grijpstra with a carefully typed list.

"The actual stuff is at Headquarters, adjutant, but this is what we found on him. Wallet, pocketknife, clean handkerchief, and so forth."

"Any money in the wallet?"

"Oh yes, plenty. Notes, cash, credit cards, checkbook, a foreign checkbook, I believe."

Grijpstra nodded at de Gier. "You hear, sergeant? Money. He wasn't even robbed. I tell you, he *fell* into that car. Nobody interfered with him."

"Yes," de Gier said tonelessly.

"You don't agree?"

"No. Look at the corpse again, closely."

Grijpstra walked back into the refrigerated room. The attendant pulled out the large metal drawer. Grijpstra shivered.

"Cold, eh?" the attendant asked. "I'm used to it, and it's nice during summer."

"I'm not cold."

"You recognize him?" de Gier asked from the far corner of the room.

Grijpstra rubbed his chin. "Yes. I didn't before. That's the man who came into Café Beelema on Saturday. We thought he was drunk. Maybe the ulcer was bothering him already."

"I watched him go into Hotel Oberon, after he staggered out of the café."

"Ah," Grijpstra said and continued to rub his chin. "I see. Fat German who owns Mercedes stays at Oberon. So does Jim Boronski. Mr. Boronski is dead in fat German's car. We'd better do something. *You'd* better do something. Find that German. Ask him questions. He's a foreigner without a fixed address and if he won't answer you satisfactorily, you can arrest him. Why don't you do that? Bring him over to Headquarters. By that time I'll have gone through the dead man's papers. You want to see the maggots?"

"Please!" de Gier said, withdrawing farther into his corner.

Grijpstra pulled the next drawer. He didn't look long. As he stepped away, the attendant pushed the drawer back into the wall.

"Did you see them?"

"Just the eggs, clusters in the corners of her mouth, as the doctor said. She's pretty, all right, although corpses never are, really. They're too dead."

"How old?"

"Hard to say. How young, rather. Nineteen, twenty-five, somewhere in between."

"Death," the attendant said. "I was reading about a place: Calcutta. Up there they have men like me who deal with the dead. They've got a name which I forget. They have long hair and a loincloth and when they don't work, they meditate. They sit quietly and reflect on the nonsense of it all. When they work, they burn fires and put the dead on the firewood, carefully, it's a ceremony, every movement has to be right. There are vultures to help the men, they're always there too. They get what falls out of the fire maybe, and they pick through the ashes. It's a better system than what we have. Here it's all mechanical. When the corpses are here awhile and nobody has come and the police don't care, they're cleared out and blasted in a huge oven with pressured fire. It should be done slowly, I think, with care, and there should be birds about."

"Crows and sea gulls," Grijpstra said. "We saw what they do a few days back. You take the car, sergeant, I'll walk. Don't be too long."

Grijpstra thought as he walked. He now knew that the stomach cramps he had been suffering from wouldn't be caused by ulcers. Mrs. Grijpstra was the way she was and had been so for a great many years. He concluded that ulcers could be avoided if nothing is relied on. If there are no points of reference, the framework the mind rests on cannot be destroyed, for there is no framework. He also knew that Jim Boronski died of natural causes; there should be no reason to pursue the search or even start it. However, the German and Boronski lived in the same hotel and they used the same car, be it for different purposes. Grijpstra saw a terrace with a view of a busy thoroughfare. He found a chair and ordered coffee. He promised himself a ten-minute rest while the trusty sergeant worked.

But he can't be trusted, he thought, for he is without his drug. Perhaps Asta would look after him. He remembered that Asta couldn't be trusted either. He forgot his fears while he watched young girls crossing the street, with sharply outlined bodies dressed in tight jeans or in narrow frocks, not quite narrow enough for the wind not to play with.

The adjutant had either picked the wrong place or the wrong time, for suddenly the crossing girls were all fat. He looked at the surrounding buildings and didn't like them either, they were square and gray. The sky was gray too. He sipped his coffee, put the cup down, and closed his eyes. Once again he saw himself bestowing the divine gift on de Gier. He wondered how the sergeant would react to his new companion.

The vision faded, and he got up and found canals and narrow streets lined with old and stately gable houses that rested his mind. He stopped to scratch a cat, spoke to a dog which changed its snarl into a pathetic grin, and picked up a shopping bag dropped by an old lady. While he listened to her complaint about rising prices, he saw the dead face of Jim Boronski again. It hadn't been a pleasant face, although the man was undoubtedly handsome. A villain, Grijpstra thought, and forgot the definition as he had to jump for his life to avoid a careening truck.

3

The address where Asta lived turned out to be a boarding house. The landlady directed the sergeant to the top floor, but when he got there, he had forgotten on which door he should knock. The second, he thought. There was no answer, and he opened the door. He was in a large bathroom and Asta was in the bath on her knees adjusting the faucets, her small, round bottom faced him. She looked over her shoulder.

"Excuse me," de Gier said, "I'll wait downstairs."

He went down and waited awhile, constructing theories to pass the time. None of the possibilities would hold. Why would the fat German kill expatriate Boronski, temporarily back in the old country? Were they businessmen fighting over a deal? What sort of a deal warrants violent death? Were they lovers of the same woman? Why would the German dump his enemy's body in his own Mercedes and then report the car as stolen? The ulcer seemed to rule out all thought of murder, but there were still mysterious and accusing facts. He left the building, bought chewing gum, chewed for a while, spat the gum out, and rang the bell again.

"Third door on the left, sir, but the ladies in this house are not supposed to have male visitors."

"Yes," de Gier said and ran up the stairs. The painful need of nicotine made him forget to knock. He saw Asta in the middle of the room. She still had no clothes on. She was on her knees again, looking over her shoulder into a mirror.

"Excuse me," de Gier said.

The girl jumped up, snatched a towel from the bed, and wrapped her slight body in it.

"For heaven's sake, don't you ever knock?"

"I did the first time, but the water of the bath was running."

"Are you wondering about my strange position?"

"Yes."

"I wanted to know what I look like when I'm on my hands and knees and somebody looks at me from the rear."

"Oh."

"What do I look like from the rear?"

"Nice."

She sighed. "Nice? Is that all?"

"Very nice," de Gier said patiently. "Appetizing. Irresistible. Please dress. The adjutant is waiting at Headquarters for his new detective and we have to see that German. I'll wait outside."

"You'll wait right here. You've seen everything already, but I would prefer you to look out of the window while I dress. What should I put on? I've never worked out of uniform. A dress? Jeans and a blouse?"

"A dress, Hotel Oberon is a classy place."

"Shouldn't you be wearing a tie then?"

"I never wear a tie. Hurry up."

"I like the way you wear your clothes," Asta said while her cotton dress rustled. "A scarf is elegant, you're an elegant man; they are rare in the police, I've never seen one except you. Even Sergeant Jurriaans isn't elegant."

"You like him, do you?"

"Yes."

"Is it true that the two of you went out one night and got drunk and that you stripped on a table and played on an Oriental rug with a girlfriend?"

"*What?*"

"Is it true?"

"Who told you that?"

"I heard," de Gier said.

"Me and Sergeant Jurriaans?"

"That's right."

"I had a drink with him once; he came into Beelema's and was distraught. He had a fight with his wife. I know his wife, she's charming. Jurriaans can be grumpy at times. He shouldn't talk about his private life to another woman, but I didn't mind."

"You didn't go anywhere with him?"

"No."

"Would you have liked to?"

She held his shoulders and pushed him round. "Of course. I love him. I would do anything for him. Even dance on tables and play on rugs."

"With another lady?"

"If he wanted me to. Shall we go? I'm ready."

De Gier was uncomfortable, but the ride didn't take long. The German wasn't in the hotel but pushed his bulk through the revolving glass door as they were ready to leave an invitation for him to come to Headquarters.

"Police? I don't want to speak to the police. Or is it about my car? Did you find my car?"

De Gier's German was slow and painful; the fat man didn't understand until Asta helped out. Her German wasn't much better than the sergeant's, but her pronunciation was better.

"We found the car, but we have to speak with you. Take us to your room."

The room was spacious and well furnished. The German didn't offer them chairs, although he sat down himself. He opened a thermos flask and filled its cup with lemonade.

"You found my car, where is it?"

"Do you know Mr. Boronski, Jim Boronski?"

"Yes. No. What is that to you?"

"What is your name? Show us your passport." De Gier found it impossible to be polite to the man. He caught the passport the German threw at him and opened it. "Karl Müller. What is your profession?"

"My firm imports wood. I buy from Mr. Boronski. He ships me wood from Colombia and Peru. We are men who do business together, no more."

"Mr. Boronski was found dead in your car this morning."

"What?"

De Gier looked at Asta.

"*Tot,*" Asta said, "in your car."

Herr Müller's pudgy red hands trembled. He replaced the flask and cup on a side table.

"*Tot, Herr Boronski tot?*"

"Quite dead."

"How did he die? Was he murdered?"

"We don't know yet. We came to ask you if you knew anything."

Müller's cheeks trembled. Sweat ran down his face. He tried to say something but the words stuck in his throat. De Gier pushed his chair closer.

"He died during the night. Where were you last night?"

"I was out. In a bar and a club. I came home late."

"How late?"

"Two o'clock maybe, or a little later."

"You remember where you were?"

"Yes."

"Write down the names of the establishments and the times you were there."

While Müller wrote, de Gier considered the next move. The man's answers were acceptable so far. There was no charge, for if the doctor was right, Boronski wasn't murdered. Müller's passport seemed to be in order. To attempt to arrest the man might cause all sorts of unpleasantness. He looked at the passport again. The man originated in Hamburg. They might check with the Hamburg police.

He took the slip of paper from the table and read the names of the bar and the club. He knew the bar, a fairly respectable place. The club was a sex club, expensive and supposedly high-class. He had never been there and couldn't remember if the place had ever figured in police reports. If Müller said that he'd been there, he was probably speaking the truth.

"I'll have to hold your passport, and I must ask you not to leave this hotel until you hear from us. Tell us all you know about Mr. Boronski."

"Shall I make notes?" Asta asked.

"Please do."

The girl crossed her legs and pointed her ball pen at a new notebook. De Gier smiled and looked away. She had slender legs and slim ankles.

Müller seemed to have come through his crisis and talked easily. He had corresponded with Boronski's firm in Bogotá, Colombia, for years and done regular business with him ever since he began importing wood from that part of the world. Gradually the shipments had grown to sizable proportions, and as even larger deals were envisaged, he had thought that he should meet his supplier. Boronski said that he would go to Amsterdam and they had agreed to stay at the same hotel.

"So you came here specially to meet him?"

No, Müller also had other business in Amsterdam.

"What do you know about Boronski's private life?"

Not much. Boronski wasn't married, had no relatives in Holland, and hadn't been to Holland for many years. He drove a Porsche that he had just bought and meant to take back to Colombia.

Was there anything wrong with him physically?

Yes, he complained about stomachaches.

Did he drink a lot?

Yes, but not to the point of getting very drunk.

Girlfriends?

Not that Müller knew of.

Visiting sex clubs?

Yes.

Had he been seeing a doctor?

Müller didn't know.

Could Müller show any correspondence with Boronski's firm?

No, not here. Müller claimed that the correspondence was on file in his office in Hamburg.

"Where is my car?" Müller asked.

De Gier explained where the car was. "You can have it back. It was shorted and the lock of the trunk was forced, but the door lock wasn't. Did you forget?"

Müller nodded. "I forgot to lock the door. In Amsterdam they steal everything. Bad city, bad food, too expensive."

"You should have stayed home."

"Can I go and pick up my car?"

"Yes, you can move within the city as long as you leave a note at the hotel desk to say where we can find you."

"When do I get my passport back?"

"Soon."

"I was planning to leave. You'll have to pay for any extra time I have to stay at the hotel."

"Let's go," de Gier said and held the door open for Asta. He left without saying goodbye, closing the door behind him with a little too much force.

"A pig," Asta said. "Shall we make inquiries about Boronski at the desk?"

The hotel manager let them into his private office and ordered coffee. He was both polite and precise.

"Mr. Boronski? Dead? How unfortunate."

"Very. He lived in Colombia and had no relatives. It may be difficult for you to collect his bill."

"Perhaps, but it's a risk of the trade."

"Did he do anything that caused special notice?"

"Yes," the manager said, "on several occasions, he bothered us and I contemplated asking him to leave. There was that business with the girl and the trouble about his car. He seemed very upset, and in pain too. I suggested he should see a doctor. There was something wrong with his stomach."

De Gier sat up. "Trouble with a lady. Would you explain?"

"Of course. When was it? Last Thursday, I believe, or Wednesday. It'll be in the register. A lady checked in. I was at the desk that night, I remember her well, a rather lovely lady. She just wanted to stay the night, well dressed, good-quality suitcase, demure, didn't say much, didn't have a credit card, so she paid cash in advance. That night I wasn't on duty, I left shortly after she arrived. The night staff reported in the morning that there had been trouble with Mr. Boronski. A strange tale indeed. It seemed that he tried to get into her room, did get into her room, in fact, and somehow bothered her."

"Attempted rape?" de Gier asked.

"No, no. I tell you, it's a strange tale. He claimed that she was in his room, that he knew her, that he had arranged with her that she would stay the night with him, and the lady claimed that she had never set eyes on the man. She phoned the desk, my assistant went up. Boronski had lost all self-control, man was foaming at the mouth, I believe, and then my assistant discovered that Boronski's room was next door. Quite an upheaval. The lady was so upset that she packed her bag and left. My assistant tried to reassure her and offered excuses, free breakfast and so forth, drinks, anything she liked, but she insisted."

"Did she get her money back?"

"Oh yes."

"And Boronski?"

"He came to see me the next morning and stated that his room had been switched in some devilish manner, for all his belongings were arranged precisely as he had left them, but they were in the other room. I didn't believe him, of course. I even showed him the register. He had room 14, not 12, he had room 14 from the start. Boronski also told me that the lady had been in his room that afternoon. He had met her in the street somewhere, she was a prostitute. The, eh, meeting was most satisfactory and she had promised to come back in the evening at ten. He went to his room before ten and she was there all right but she didn't know him."

"Wouldn't somebody here have noticed her in the company of Mr. Boronski?"

The manager hid a yawn behind a dainty hand. De Gier noticed that he had polished fingernails.

"Excuse me, no, nobody noticed; we have sixty-four rooms here, there's a lot of coming and going."

"How could she have got into his room? Boronski had the key, didn't he?"

The manager yawned again. "Do excuse me, I haven't had much sleep lately. I wouldn't know."

"Amazing," de Gier said. "You also mentioned other trouble, something about a car?"

"Yes, another tall tale. He came to see me and said that his car, a brand new Porsche that he had just bought, tax-free, to take with him to South America suddenly had the steering wheel *on the wrong side*. I ask you. Fortunately, I knew by then that the man wasn't in his right mind; this was after the business with the lady, you see. I didn't want to listen to him, but he practically dragged me into the street. The car was there, a lovely job, silver color, red leather upholstery, must have cost him a fortune. The registration plates were special, Colombian, must have got them through the local consulate. The steering wheel was on the right side, and he said it was on the left when he bought the car the day before. Quite impossible. To change a steering wheel is a major operation, not the sort of thing somebody does with a screwdriver and a couple of wrenches in a few minutes. This was in the morning. He said he had parked the car in front of the hotel, had worked in his room for an hour, come out, and noticed the change. He had phoned the agent where he bought the car and the agent confirmed that the wheel was on the left side. So Boronski said he wanted me to phone the agent but I refused. I didn't want to listen to him. It was his car and his mind. We only provide rooms and meals." The manager laughed. "Anyway, the next day the wheel was back in its correct position so the mishap was taken care of."

De Gier gaped. Asta stopped writing.

"Did I hear you correctly?" de Gier asked. "Or am I going mad too?"

"You heard me correctly, but the man was mad."

"Did you see the car again?"

"No. He wanted to show it to me, but I refused to leave the desk. Damn it all, I'm not a psychiatrist, I'm a hotel manager. There had been all the other nonsense too. His watch disappeared from his bathroom and turned up an hour later in the spot where it should have been all the time. He sent his clothes for dry cleaning and the wrong clothes came back to his room. One of the girls checked, but by that time they had changed into the right clothes again. Mr. Boronski was suffering from some form of paranoia. He hallucinated. He was physically ill too, he complained of stomach cramps and we had to serve him porridge for dinner; he exhausted the room service waiter by phoning for milk every half hour. I'm glad he has left us."

"Yes," de Gier said.

"I'm sorry he is dead, of course, sergeant. Now if there is anything else I can help you with." The manager looked at his watch. "I'm afraid I . . ."

De Gier got up. "Thank you."

Asta stumbled in the corridor, the sergeant stooped to catch her arm, and she turned and kissed him on the mouth.

"Hey!"

"I've been wanting to do that, do you mind?"

"No."

"Kiss me again."

"You kissed me. I don't kiss colleagues during working hours. Would you like coffee?"

They sat in the coffee shop of the hotel for a while.

Asta served the sergeant, she even stirred his coffee for him. He grinned.

"You're a slave. I thought that young ladies don't do that sort of thing anymore."

"What sort of thing?"

"Be servile."

"I love to be servile," Asta whispered. "I'm old-fashioned. I like to be on my back and the man to be on me. I like to oblige. It's a pity you have nothing to carry, I would carry it for you, even if it was very heavy."

"Have you had many men?"

She pursed her thick lower lip and a tiny frown appeared on her smooth forehead. She blew at a curl that hung in her eyes.

"Hmm. Not too many. I tried some young men but they weren't any good, too quick. The older men are usually married, and when they embrace me, I know that they're looking at their watch behind my neck. I can see it in their eyes. They're slow and polite, but they go away when it's over. You wouldn't be like that, would you?"

"I might be. Who did you believe, the manager or Boronski?"

"Boronski."

"Why?"

"I saw his corpse, remember," Asta said. "I didn't like him at all, not with that low forehead and the eyes too close together. I've known men with low foreheads and close eyes that I liked, but Boronski had something nasty about him. But he wouldn't lie like that. And that manager didn't really exist, did you notice that?"

"How do you mean?"

"He was just like the hotel. It looks all right, but once you're in it you can see that it's all hollow.

They have tried to recapture the dignity of the past; they've got the right architecture and the right trimmings, but there's nothing in it. Everything is hollow, filled with air. He was too. He's like a doll I once had. I threw it away. Even when I scratched its face and tore its clothes, it wasn't there."

"How do we find out who told us the truth?"

She giggled. De Gier looked up. The giggle was vulgar. It reminded him of the cry of a disheveled parrot in the city's zoo. He would always spend a few moments with it when he strayed into the zoo. The parrot was a jolly common bird, quite unlike its splendid mates eyeing the passing crowd arrogantly from their high perches. So far Asta had impressed him as refined, different from the other policewomen he had worked with.

"Are you testing me or don't you know how to find out whether Boronski saw things that weren't there?"

"Let's say I'm testing you," de Gier said.

She reached into her bag and gave him her notebook and her pen. "No. Write the solution down and fold the paper, then I'll tell you what I suggest doing and we'll see if we have the same solution."

He wrote while she looked the other way. "Okay. Tell me what we do."

"Boronski must have parked his Porsche close to the hotel. We'll find it and see which side the steering wheel is on. We know that it had the wheel on the right side when the manager saw it. If it's on the other side now, Boronski spoke the truth."

"Right," de Gier said.

"Can I see what you wrote?"

"No." He crumpled the paper and put it in his pocket.

"Am I right?"

"Let's find the car."

They found the car a few blocks away on the Princes-canal. It had two traffic tickets under the windshield wiper. De Gier made a note of its location, phoned Headquarters from the nearest booth, and told them to tow it away. The car's steering wheel was on the left side.

4

Their eyes are the same color, Grijpstra thought as he watched the communication between the commissaris and the girl. He still referred to her as the girl, and the memory of the divine vision wherein he had given her to de Gier was clear in his mind. The sunlit antique room which the commissaris used as an office should have comforted him, as it had done so many times when the detectives discussed a case under the benevolent guidance of their chief, but it didn't now. At first he felt good again and easily fell into his role as an archangel handing out a sublimely beautiful girl to a special mortal, his cherished friend. The adjutant mused, and sucked on his cigar, which tasted bad but cost too much to throw away. The spotlight of the vision veered away from Asta, whose crossed legs showed enough of her thighs to stimulate Grijpstra's carnal appetite which he had transferred so successfully to the sergeant, to the pond that had formed part of his original fantasy. At that time, the pond was filled with various animal shapes, pleasurably engaged in play. He could see them more clearly now. There were monstrosities. A reptilian bird had caught something that might be a squirrel but had the legs of a frog. There was an evil glint in the bird's eye; it was relishing the frantic movements of its helpless prey. A winged fish was about to leave the water to attack a many-headed bird of splendor preparing to drink from the water that was no longer clear. Another shape, partly fish, partly animal, with a hooded head, floated about, engaged in reading a small book, a book of spells and curses, Grijpstra assumed, as he tried to read the text. He shook himself and tuned in to the conversation.

"So we have an indication," the commissaris said, "a concrete fact we may call it. Very good of you, Asta, we should be grateful to Sergeant Jurriaans for lending you to us. You saved us some work, although I think that the value of Boronski's other accusations should be ascertained as well. Perhaps the sergeant can go back to the hotel this evening and find out what name the lady used when she registered. It may be her true name, and that part of Boronski's tale may be untrue, although if one part of his nightmare connects with reality, the others may . . . It was you who suggested finding the car, wasn't it, Asta?"

"Excuse me, sergeant," Asta said and got up. She walked over to where he sat, reached in the side pocket of his jacket and produced a crumpled piece of paper. She read it and laughed.

"The sergeant was teaching me, sir. We played a game. I would say what I thought we should do and he would write his idea down. Here you are."

The commissaris read the note. *"Find the car Boronski referred to."*

"I see." He took off his glasses, blew on them, and rubbed them gently with his handkerchief. "But you shouldn't protect him, dear." He turned to de Gier. "And you shouldn't be smiling. You've been in the game a long time. Credit is . . . Grijpstra, you had a good term for credit, what is it again?"

"A fart in a brown paper bag, sir."

"Exactly. However, we have the Porsche and the hotel manager's statement. We also have a corpse, dead of disease but found in the trunk of a car with the lid down. What else?"

"An obnoxious German, sir," de Gier said.

"Ah yes. I'm glad you qualify him, for there are also good Germans. I mention the point, because it has taken me a long time to admit the existence of intelligent, sensitive, and highly developed Germans. During the war I tended to forget, to my loss, I might say. But we haven't *got* the man. There's no charge. Are you planning to find confirmation of his whereabouts last night?"

"I thought I might go to the nightclub and the bar."

"Can I go, sir?" Asta asked.

The commissaris looked at the slight figure of the girl. He hesitated. Asta's lips pouted. "I'm not as weak as I look."

He nodded. "I know. Sergeant Jurriaans told me, and I heard what you did to the dog at Beelema's. Very well, you can go if you like. In which case Grijpstra can visit the hotel again and de Gier can stay here. There should be a telex from the Hamburg police, I've asked them to give us any information they may have on Herr Müller. If there's nothing out of the ordinary there, sergeant, you'll have to return his passport. I don't believe in unnecessarily annoying civilians, especially not if they are our guests. I should have an early night, my wife tells me. You can wait here for the reply from Germany and your colleagues can report back to you if anything turns up so that you can plan further actions. Now." He opened a drawer of his desk and held up a wallet.

"I went through the contents of Boronski's wallet. There is a fair amount of cash, here are his credit cards, and there is an alphabetical register of names and phone numbers, mostly in Colombia and Peru, it seems, and some here in Europe. Mr. Müller is included—there is an office number and a private number, so we may assume that the two men had fairly intimate dealings with each other. There are no photographs except one which the photo room was kind enough to duplicate. It's rather small and in black and white, but I would like to study it closely. The photo room provided me with a slide, which I will now project; would Asta perhaps draw the curtains?"

The commissaris busied himself with a projector, and Grijpstra set up a screen. The projection was life-size. It showed a treeless busy street with wide sidewalks. Boronski and a female companion, arms linked, were walking toward the camera; around them were several men in black suits and with dark faces. Street sellers were selling trinkets from shoddy suitcases. Dirty children ran in front of the couple.

"Taken by a street photographer," de Gier said.

"That's what I thought, sergeant. This must be in South America. Please remember that it was the only photograph in the wallet, so Boronski valued it. What do you think of the lady? Study her at your leisure."

The room became silent for a full minute.

"What do you think? Ladies first. Asta?"

"The lady is Dutch, sir. I'm sure of it. The skirt she is wearing is expensive, but it was on sale in Amsterdam two months ago. It's tweed, I remember the C&A stores advertising it. Strange that she would wear tweed in South America; isn't Colombia a warm country?"

"Yes, but Bogotá has a cool climate. I looked it up in my encyclopedia this afternoon. The city is nine thousand feet high and usually chilly. Are you sure about that skirt, constable?"

"Absolutely, sir, the lady is wearing the complete combination C&A advertised. The vest goes with the skirt and is of a special cut, it's called the Groninger style. Originally the style was for men only, but C&A launched it for women. Even the blouse fits the prescribed combination."

"I would also say the woman is Dutch, sir," de Gier said. "She is about thirty years old and still slim, but she'll soon be heavy and she has a local face. Maybe it's the hair style, but it's also the features."

"What do you think, Grijpstra?"

"She's married, sir. I see the wedding ring, thick, gold, without a stone. An old-fashioned wedding ring on her left hand, that is, if the photograph isn't reversed. Is the traffic on the left or on the right side in Colombia?"

"I don't know. In the photograph the cars drive on the right."

"Right-hand traffic," de Gier said. "I saw a list of left-hand traffic countries, Colombia wasn't on it."

"Good. We know that Boronski isn't married, Herr Müller told us. So this would be an affair. Affairs are quite common but we might try to find out who the woman is. Bogotá is a big city with two million inhabitants, but I don't think there will be too many of our countrymen over there. I can try our embassy out there; I could also try the police, but I hear that it's hard to establish contact with them. We had some illegal Colombian immigrants the other day who had fallen afoul of the law and we couldn't raise any information at all. I'll see if I can contact somebody on the teletyper, perhaps the Ministry of Foreign Affairs can assist; they've been helpful before. Anything else you noticed?"

"Yes," Asta said, "I think I see something. The woman is in love. The man isn't. She is good looking, he's showing her off, but he only wants to bed her and be rid of her again." The girl's voice was flat but trembled slightly on the last part of her sentence. The room became silent.

"Very well," the commissaris said, "you can open the curtains again, dear."

De Gier helped the commissaris to rearrange the projector into its case, and Grijpstra rolled up the screen. The commissaris limped to the door.

"How's your leg, sir?"

"Worse," the commissaris said, "and it shouldn't be in summer. The heat usually stops the pain. And I have my wife after me, she wants me to rest; maybe I should listen to her."

Asta and de Gier had left.

"What do you think of this case, sir?"

"What do I know, Grijpstra? I haven't seen the corpse, I'm not doing my job well these days. What do *you* think?" He closed the door and indicated a chair. "I have a few more minutes before my wife will call."

"Do you know the morgue attendant who is called Jacobs, sir?"

"Yes. He has been with the morgue a long time, but he's often ill. The man survived Auschwitz. It's strange that he selected such a morbid profession after all he went through. He came back alone, all his relatives died. Did you meet him today? I'm glad he is sane again, he was institutionalized for a while."

"He was talking about the dead this morning, sir, when we investigated the corpse. The way he talked interested me. He said that the dead sometimes hang about the morgue and are frightened, and that he talks to them and tries to reassure them and send them on their way. I went to see him again, just before I came here. The morgue is close and there was something I wanted to ask him."

Grijpstra fumbled with a cigar. The commissaris flicked his lighter and waited.

"I didn't like that corpse, sir. I've always paid special attention to corpses, it's part of the job; usually you get some sort of impression that's helpful. Do you remember the case of the blond baboon, sir?"

"Yes. Mrs. Carnet?"

"Yes. She looked victorious, as if she had pulled something off, just before she was killed. There have been other cases where the corpse hinted at something. This Boronski was different, he died of natural causes, but I had a distinct impression of evil, secretive evil, extreme egotism. There was also fear, but you feel that with most corpses. Nobody is courageous when it's all over and he is about to enter the unknown."

"So you went back to Jacobs? Why?"

"I wanted to know what he felt about the corpse."

"Did he tell you?"

"Yes. He said it was giving him trouble. He said Boronski was still around in the morgue; hating, cursing, frantic with rage."

"Was Jacobs bothered by that?"

"Not too much. He had protected himself." Grijpstra

smiled. "He said he had made a transparent egg around himself, and that Boronski's spirit wouldn't be able to get through it. He said he always makes the egg when he has a troublesome client. I found him in his little office, peacefully sucking on a pipe and reading some holy book in Hebrew."

"Jacobs is a wise man," the commissaris said.

Grijpstra lumbered to the door. He turned before he left. "You know that we haven't really got a case. We are chasing phantoms again, just as we did during the weekend, but this time de Gier insists on going on."

"Are you with him, adjutant?"

"I am, sir."

"Good. The sergeant is developing, but he should still be watched."

Grijpstra walked back to his office and addressed the empty corridor. "I'm with him," he said loudly, "but I overdo it. I've even given him the loveliest girl I've seen in a long time, a girl, moreover, who prefers men my age to men his age. Now she's all his, to mess up as he likes."

He got into the open elevator, didn't pay attention, and went all the way round before he got off at the proper floor.

He was still mumbling. "A lovely girl with the right perversion. A pearl, for a pig."

He forced himself to think of something else and evoked the thought of hot water and a sharp razor. He found his shaving gear in his desk drawer and walked over to the rest room. Ah, to shave at ease, for there wasn't much to do, just a leisurely walk to Hotel Oberon to find out what the woman's name might be and another pleasant walk back to Headquarters to check her with the computer.

Then his mood changed again. He no longer saw the

smooth lines the shaver traced through bubbly foam but the pond that had been in his vision when he was an angel, giving Asta away. The pond was filled with murky water now and sinister tiny animals tore at each other in the greenish slime. The sight unnerved him, the shaver caught his skin and a thick trickle of blood formed a fat drop and stained his shirt.

5

Managers are all the same, Asta thought as she sat opposite the man in an office that could have been any office. The man was still looking at her police card. His face was blank.

"I'm a police officer, as you can see. The photograph is of my face, right? I'm not here to apply for a position in this establishment, I'm here to find out whether a certain Mr. Karl Müller, a fat German businessman, came here last night and I want you to tell me at what time he arrived and at what time he left."

"Yes," the man said.

They make them in a machine, she thought. The other one ran a hotel, this one runs a brothel. They are employees, there are others behind them who may be alive. This man isn't. He either came out of the metal mouth of some fantastic gadget or he grew in a big bowl of warm fluid. When he was done they fished him out, dried him, put him on his legs, slipped him into a plastic envelope, and brought him here. He was already programmed so nothing could go wrong. All he has to do is greet the visiting lechers, take their money, pour them full of alcohol, and steer them to the right girl. I don't fit his formula, and he doesn't know what to do now.

"Are you alone?" the man asked.

"Yes, but don't get any ideas. If you touch me, I'll tie you into a knot with both your feet in your mouth."

The man smiled. "Really?"

Asta smiled too. "Really. Now will you tell me about that German or do you want me to get help? I trust your license is in order. If it is, I could still charge you with living on the profit of prostitution of another person or persons, that article hasn't been revoked, you know. We still use it occasionally."

"Quite," the man said. "I'm sorry, officer. I have been trying to remember that German you mentioned. We had a busy night yesterday, there's a convention in the hotel across the street, of politicians. We were a bit crowded. Quite a few of the gentlemen were fat, and some of them were German. Müller, you said the name was?"

"Karl Müller, man in his forties, obese, bald on top and a long fringe below, a lot of gold teeth, a heavy gold watch, light-color suit and a red tie."

"Ah. Yes. I remember the tie. Red is my favorite color. Let me check the credit card slips."

He opened a neat file and turned small rectangular slips, wetting his finger.

"Here we are, Karl Müller, the address is in Hamburg. Yes, I remember him. He complained, the girl hadn't been cooperative, he wanted a discount. I asked the girl what was wrong and she said she refused to get into the bath with him. The more expensive rooms have baths, you see, with gold-plated faucets, special feature of the house. The baths are king size; even so, there was little room left for the girl. He also complained about the quality of our snacks, we serve free snacks with the drinks. They're good. I've never had anybody criticizing them before."

"What time did he leave?"

The manager closed the file and placed it on the right corner of his desk, tapping it with his finger so that it was parallel to one side and perpendicular to the other.

"He left early. He wanted another girl, but we had so many clients that the girls could make their own choice, and nobody wanted him. Sometimes I'm able to obtain free-lance help but usually not on Mondays; the ladies are resting then after the weekend. I made a few unsuccessful phone calls and the gentleman left."

"What time?"

"Hard to say, there was so much coming and going. Around midnight, I would think."

"You'll have to sign a statement to that effect, and I also need a statement from the girl who wouldn't get into the bath. She'll have to confirm the time he left."

The manager puffed on his cigarette. His eyes evaded the demon that was pestering him.

"I'm afraid that will be impossible."

"As you like," Asta said. "Let me use your phone. I don't care how many sex clubs there are in Amsterdam, they're still illegal. I'm going to get my sergeant and some uniformed cops and we'll go through the place. Don't leave this room until my colleagues have arrived."

There were two telephones on the desk; the smaller model was pseudoantique. He picked it up.

"Ask Willemine to come into my office, will you? It's urgent, I don't care if she is busy."

The knife flashed past Asta and hit the center of the circle that had been painted on the cupboard door. De

Gier walked from the other side of the room to retrieve it.

"You might have hit me," Asta said.

"No, I missed you by a foot. I'm accurate within an inch, and I've been practicing for a year. I've always been bad with knives. Grijpstra is better, he's never more than a centimeter off, but he is slow on the draw. That part I've got right, I think, you didn't see me draw the knife, did you?"

"No."

"Good, but not good enough. Your results aren't good enough either. So Müller left the club at midnight, two hours earlier than he told us. The difference doesn't constitute a crime. He had been drinking, didn't know what the time was. We still can't arrest the slob. What happened to Grijpstra?"

"Here," Grijpstra said. The knife came again. Grijpstra took off his jacket and hung it on the knife. "I've been to the hotel; the girl we're looking for gave a false name. It isn't in the computer. The address she gave is in Rotterdam. I telephoned the police there, and a patrol car drove to the street; the street exists but the number doesn't."

"Harassment," de Gier said, "and she had help inside the hotel. Boronski must have stayed in room 12. Did you check the register?"

"Yes. The entries are made with pencil. The pencil hadn't been pressed down and the handwriting wasn't too clear. It's easy to change a 2 into a 4. I took the register with me and the lab looked at it. They say that the 2 of 12 may have been erased and replaced by a 4, but they won't swear to it."

De Gier took Grijpstra's jacket off the knife and hung it on a hook. He replaced the knife in a sheath that had been sewn to the lining of his jacket.

"Inside help, probably the same person who changed

Boronski's dry-cleaned clothes and then changed them again; he or she must also have lifted his watch from the bathroom and replaced it."

Grijpstra walked over to a battered set of drums and picked up two tapered sticks. He played on the side of the largest drum, lightly hitting the center in the middle and at the end of each bar.

"No," Asta said. "Do you often do that here, play drums?"

"Ever since the lost and found department gave him the drums," de Gier said. "Grijpstra gets everything free, I had to pay for this flute." He had taken the flute from his desk and blew a single note. Grijpstra sat up and started a fairly complicated rhythm. Asta couldn't hear who followed whom. The music seemed to become more intricate. The two men played for no more than five minutes. De Gier dropped the flute back into his desk, Grijpstra finished the way he had begun, with slowing taps on the side of the main drum.

"Wow! What was it? An improvisation?"

"Of course," Grijpstra said. "Ibaniz composed this for piano. He never thought of us, we can't play the piano."

Asta shook her head. "Sergeant Jurriaans told me that you two are musicians, but I never believed him. Most of what he says isn't connected with daily life."

"I should hope so," de Gier said. The telephone rang. "Right, I'll come and pick it up."

He was back within minutes, waving paper. "Hear this. In German but I'll try to translate it. *Karl Müller, businessman, import and export of lumber, apart from legitimate business possibly active in unproved drug dealing on large scale. Please let us know immediately if you can produce charge. Hamburg Police, Criminal Investigation Department, Narcotics Branch, signed Inspector Hans Wingel.*"

Grijpstra read the teletype message and gave it to Asta. He began to pace the room.

"So now we have some sort of construction. Ever since I heard that Jim Boronski lived in Colombia, I suspected drugs. We know that the stuff coming from Turkey is being intercepted too often, and the supply is irregular anyway. Colombia is a new source that seems more efficient, and the hashish and marihuana that originates there is of good quality. The Colombians also sell cocaine, and cocaine ranks about as high as heroin, in price, that is. A smart man like Boronski and another smart man like Müller would prefer to deal in cocaine; just a few pounds make a golden deal. So now let's assume that Boronski played foul and that Müller got annoyed. He harasses Boronski to the point where he drops dead."

"In Müller's car," de Gier said.

"RIGHT!" shouted Grijpstra. "That's where we go wrong. Every time. The whole silly thing is impossible. Boronski is sick, he gets sicker, he dies. That's all we have. We should close the case and go home. There's no logic in it. See you tomorrow." He put on his jacket and stamped out of the room.

"I haven't got a car," said de Gier, "but I could walk you home. You'll be safe, your landlady doesn't approve of male visitors."

"You can kiss me here."

De Gier bent down and kissed her.

"Is that the way you kiss? Just smack?"

She embraced him. "Can't you bend your knees? Or shall I stand on a chair?"

"No."

"All right, I'll take *you* home. My car is only two blocks from here and you live in the southside of the city; you have no car and it's a long bus ride."

"Who told you that?"

"Sergeant Jurriaans. I know that you are single and that you live with a cat in a luxurious apartment and that you have no current girlfriend."

"I'm married, I have four kids, and my wife worries about me."

"No."

"Didn't you say that Jurriaans can't be trusted?"

She opened the door. "Let's go, darling."

The car was an old compact Ford, battered and rusty. The inside was cluttered with clothes, cartons of cigarettes, and frayed wicker baskets containing odd objects. She made room on the passenger seat. The dashboard was cluttered too. A faded cloth tiger was glued to the loudspeaker. De Gier counted three boxes of tissues of different brands, all opened.

"How can you look so neat when you drive about in this junk pile?"

"Different parts of my mind manifest themselves in different ways. There's nothing wrong with this car, everything works."

She drove fast and paid little attention to traffic lights. De Gier hardly noticed. Her hand was on his shoulder. I'm in love, he thought. I haven't been in love for years. It's as if I knew the girl since the day I began my first life. He looked at the tiger, rooted solidly in the framework of the loudspeaker. Maybe we hunted sabertoothed tigers together when we were still apes. This is absurd. I don't want to be in love.

"This is south, am I going the right way?"

He gave her the address. She turned through a red light and put her foot down. A patrol car's siren howled behind them. She parked in front of the apartment building. The patrol car screeched to a halt and two constables came running up. Asta got out and showed her card. De Gier got out too.

"Evening."

"Evening, sergeant."

"Are you busy tonight?" de Gier asked.

"No, sergeant. Maybe later. There's a thriller on TV, all the crooks are watching it. Maybe later we'll find something to do."

"Good hunting."

"Thank you. You wouldn't be taking this constable home for pleasure, would you, sergeant?"

"He's thinking of it, but he won't get anywhere," Asta said. "Good night."

The patrol car drove off, the constables grinned and waved.

"Would you come up for a drink?" de Gier asked.

"I would."

They drank on the balcony; it was only a small balcony, but she kept away from him. He went inside to feed his cat. The cat purred and ran to the balcony. Asta picked it up. "You're ugly, you have too many colors."

De Gier came out to water his geraniums. "She's got the colors of a Persian carpet, that's why she's called Tabriz. Can I make you a meal? I've got some noodles and frozen soup, they might go well together. I could toss a salad, too."

They ate and washed up together. De Gier thought he should be flirtatious but couldn't think of suitable words. The girl was quiet and efficient. He didn't have to tell her where to put the dishes; she opened the cupboard and found the right places.

"Coffee?" he asked.

"No, sergeant, I think I should go." She raised her head and he kissed her lightly. When he tried to embrace her, she stepped out of his arms. "No. I'll see you tomorrow."

He pulled his only easy chair onto the balcony and sat with the cat on his lap. The cat turned over and he pulled at some hair that had matted together. The cat groaned. "I won't do it if you don't want me to." The cat didn't move. He tugged. Suddenly the cat jumped away and a sizable cluster of hair stayed in his hand. "Bothered you, did it? Used me as a tool, did you? Clever Tabriz." The cat wanted to come back, but he got up. "I don't want to work, Tabriz, I want to stay here and be with you, but I think there may be something to do." He looked at the sky; heavy clouds floated toward each other. "No car and it'll be raining." He put on a round cotton hat and took the elevator down to the basement where he extracted an old bicycle out of the clutch of another.

Half an hour later, a lone cyclist entered the inner city. The dying sun touched the lining of clouds that were lowering themselves on the spires of medieval churches. He left his cycle under a tree at the Brewers-canal and became a pedestrian. The herringstall on the bridge across from Hotel Oberon was doing a brisk business. He bought a herring, liberally sprinkled with chopped onions, and retired under the awning at the side to eat it in peace.

"Evening," a portly gentleman said.

"Evening," de Gier said. "I thought you had gone home."

"I didn't. I've been here for an hour and a half. I've eaten six herrings. He hasn't come out yet. Stay here, I'll have a beer at Beelema's. I'll be right back."

6

"There," Grijpstra said.

They moved simultaneously, each taking a side of the man, keeping well back. Müller waddled ahead, carrying a flat case. It was dark by now and the ornamental street lights, spaced far apart, played with the fat man's shadow. They also played with another shadow, slim and sharp, darting in and out of the lights. The shadow was attached to a girl, dressed in faded jeans and a trim jacket, bouncing on high-heeled sneakers. De Gier, on the waterside, and Grijpstra, inconspicuously merging with the walls of small and narrow houses, lagged even farther behind. Two more shadows joined the procession; they had sneaked from a side alley. They moved as gracefully as the girl. They were tall and thin, as black as their owners, who were both in their late teens or early twenties, with shaved skulls, sporting leather jackets and tapered dungarees.

Rapists, Grijpstra thought.

Robbers, de Gier thought.

Can't have that, they both thought. Neither man was concerned about the girl's safety at that moment. They were hunting and Müller was the prey. If the boys caught up with the girl, there would be a scuffle, some noise, a scream maybe. Müller would be distracted and not do what he was supposed to do, or do it in a different manner, adding complications to the simple situation that now faced the original pursuers. One of the muggers followed the line of trees bordering the canal, the other adopted Grijpstra's tactics. Neither of them was aware of the danger behind. De Gier ran, Grijpstra lumbered. De Gier drew his knife faster than Grijpstra.

"Hey."

The boys stopped and turned. They were well trained. They did the right thing, their knives were out too, but they were at a disadvantage.

"Drop it."

The knives fell. They were light and didn't clatter much on the cobblestones.

Grijpstra's catch muttered four-letter words, the other stared at de Gier. Of the two, the adjutant's prey was the most surprised. Grijpstra could not be in the same profession as the boy, yet he was. This well-dressed elderly man with the kind face, complete with tie, cuff links and neatly folded white handkerchief in his breast pocket, was asking a black street mugger for his money. The boy's deepest mind was disturbed. Facts no longer fitted reality. There was the stiletto, its cruel point pressing against his throat, there was the hand on the shoulder of his leather jacket, there was the pleasant voice, asking for money.

The other boy could accept his particular set of circumstances more easily. The tall man in the round cotton hat looked somewhat odd. He could, if the imagination were stretched just short of the breaking point, perhaps be lurking in dark streets, prowling for loot.

"Give," Grijpstra said.

De Gier didn't speak. He hissed. He supported the boy's bare skull with his left hand, pressed the knife with the other. The skin on the boy's throat was about to break. The boy fumbled in his pocket and came out with crumpled bills. De Gier grabbed the money and swung the boy round. The boy held on to a tree while de Gier patted him down. The sergeant's foot pushed the boy's knife into the water, it splashed softly. Grijpstra picked up the other boy's knife.

"Give!"

The boy gave.

"Off with you, that way!" Grijpstra pointed over his shoulder. The other boy was running already.

There was a second splash as the other knife hit the canal's calm surface.

The detectives waited for the boys to slip into the alley that had emitted them a few moments ago and turned.

They should have kept the knives. Müller, alerted by the splashes, looked around. Asta stopped short.

"You?" Müller asked. The arm that carried his case swung back. The girl ducked and pulled her gun, aiming the pistol as it came out of her pocketbook. The pistol's click immobilized Müller.

"You're under arrest; drop your case, turn round, and hold your arms behind your back."

Asta shifted the gun to her left hand and produced her handcuffs. She had some trouble trying to fit them around Müller's fat wrists. He kicked twice, forward and backward. The case shot into the canal and Asta staggered.

When Müller turned, clawing at the air separating him from the girl, de Gier jumped. The sergeant's flat hand came down, hitting Müller in the neck. The man's thick skin and spongy blubbery tissue absorbed the impact, but de Gier hit again in a blur of vindictive fury. Müller's breath escaped in a burst of foul air; after that he sobbed. Then he fell, taking his time, spreading his monstrous body between a tree trunk and de Gier's feet. The sergeant stepped back.

Grijpstra was on his knees, holding Asta's leg.

"I'm all right," she said. "He caught me on the side. It hurts but the knee'll still work. Help me up please."

She held on to Grijpstra and hobbled over to de Gier.

"The case, it's floating away, we've got to get it. You can lower me down and I'll pick it up. Here, hold my gun."

De Gier lay down and Grijpstra held his feet. Asta grabbed the low railing at the end of the cobblestones and lowered her body gently. She touched the case with the point of her shoe and maneuvered it toward her.

"Don't drop me, sergeant." The case was between her feet. "Pull me up now."

Grijpstra handcuffed Müller while de Gier and Asta opened the case; it contained sixteen small plastic bags. Asta undid one and sniffed at the powder; she passed the bag to de Gier.

"Probably cocaine, the laboratory'll know. You did well, Asta."

She looked round. Grijpstra was slapping Müller's cheeks slowly and methodically with both hands.

"Is he coming to?"

"In a minute, not yet."

She kissed de Gier, just touching his lips. "Did I really do well? I wasn't sure. The connection between Müller and Boronski was drugs. There would be drugs in the hotel. Müller knew we were after him. He had to get rid of the evidence; he didn't want to leave it in the hotel, for we might have traced it back to him. He thought he would dump it into the canal, a little bag at a time. He would wait until dark. If I could catch him with the drug in his possession, I could arrest him. Right?"

"Wrong, you wanted to do it on your own. We never work by ourselves, not if we can help it. You should have asked me or the adjutant to assist you. We're supposed to work as a team."

"Yes, I'm sorry."

"It's a long road," de Gier whispered, "and there's nothing at the end, but we can have company on the way."

"Yes."

He saw her lower lip tremble and embraced her. She was talking, but her face pressed against his chest, and he couldn't hear what she said. He held her at arm's length. "Say that again?"

She was crying now. "Please don't think I wanted the credit of the arrest. It was that you looked so happy on your balcony with Tabriz. I thought the two of you should rest for a while. Please tell the commissaris you made the arrest."

"That's all right." He gave her her gun and his handkerchief. "Cops don't cry, not much anyway. How's he doing, Grijpstra?"

"Awake, and he wants to get up."

Together they pushed and pulled until Müller was in balance. They led him back, and Grijpstra telephoned for a car at Café Beelema. De Gier parked the wheezing Müller against the bridge railing while he bought Asta a herring. The car, a minibus driven by Karate, arrived within minutes.

"Where to, sergeant?"

"To Headquarters. Tell the turnkeys to make him comfortable. We'll interrogate him later tonight."

"Right. If you have a minute, you and the adjutant might go over to our station. Sergeant Jurriaans wants to talk to you."

"No," de Gier said, "I've had enough for tonight. Some other time."

"You'd better go, sergeant, me and the chief did a little work for you tonight."

"Tell me what you did."

"No. The chief wants to tell you himself."

The bus drove off.

Grijpstra came out of the café, wiping beer froth off his mouth.

"Why did you let that bus go? I don't want to walk back to Headquarters."

"I have my bicycle," de Gier said, "but Asta wants to go with me and it won't carry two passengers. There's also a proposition from the station here, which is around the corner. Jurriaans wants to see us."

"Good. He can have us driven home."

They walked slowly, Asta in the middle.

"See?" Asta said, pointing at a disorderly heap of feathers. "This is where the Chinese throws out his garbage, and there's nothing we can do about it. It isn't just feathers, there's blood and meat too."

"Good for rats," Grijpstra said, steering her around a temporary fence. "This part of town'll never get organized. What are they blacktopping this area for? What's wrong with cobblestones?"

Asta tried not to limp. De Gier supported her elbow.

"You realize that we are still nowhere," Grijpstra said. "So Herr Müller is a drug dealer and we can prove it. That's nice. But drugs is not our department. That the Hamburg police will be pleased has nothing to do with us either. First we had a murder and no corpse, it added up to zero. Now we have a corpse and no murder. Zero equals zero."

De Gier grinned. His arm slipped around Asta's shoulders. "There's nothing more glorious than zero, adjutant. You can multiply it at will, you can divide it at will, and it will always be the same. We can lose ourselves in nothing and go as far as we like; we'll never hit the other end of it."

The adjutant hadn't thought of a reply yet when Sergeant Jurriaans welcomed his guests with outstretched arms, beaming at the bedraggled group that reluctantly entered his small office.

7

"You look tired," Jurriaans said. "Are they overworking you already?"

Asta lit a cigarette. Her hand trembled.

"No, I fell and hurt my knee; otherwise I'm having a good time."

"How do you like de Gier?"

De Gier reached for the match Grijpstra was about to strike; he put it in his mouth.

"This is not a social call, colleague. Please come to the point."

Asta smiled. "I love him. I love you too. My soul is torn."

Jurriaans nodded. "I'd advise you to lean his way, even if he's short-tempered. Married men are easy to deal with, but they've lost their spunk; the stress of the home situation takes its toll. Married men also carry guilt which clogs up the atmosphere. Take him and come to me for comfort. I'll always be around for I can't get away."

De Gier's teeth snapped through his match and he took another from Grijpstra's hand. Grijpstra gave him his matchbox and took Jurriaans's lighter. He lit his cigar and slipped the lighter into his pocket.

"Why are we here?"

"You're here because your chase has come to an end. I've liberated you. If you like, I'll tell you about it, after you return my lighter, of course."

Grijpstra replaced the lighter.

Jurriaans sat back. He cleared his throat.

"Well, where shall I start? I can't start at the beginning, for I don't know where it is. My interference came so much later, and it wasn't even mine, for Karate saw him. He saw the Prime Punk, and we subsequently arrested him. About two hours ago I tried to get hold of you, but I couldn't trace you. I wanted you to hear the Chief Punk confess, but he'll repeat his performance if you like, and if you don't, I have his signed statement."

"Who?" Grijpstra asked.

"He is a mugger and he robs cars. He's quick and sly and an expert, but Karate was quicker. Karate and I were driving about tonight; with Ketchup on leave and Asta in the higher spheres I'm even more short-staffed than usual and besides I was bored. A bit of active duty cheers me up sometimes. We drove through the Red Mill Alley, and Karate braked and raced out of the car and confronted the Punk. He is twenty years old and leads the other Punks, the second best gang of the district. The best gang is the Black Jackets and I'm sorry we didn't catch their chief for he specializes in perfidity. The Punks will break your bones, the Black Jackets will suck the marrow. They're bad and they're black.

This is a racist station and we tend to identify the two ideas. That is a mistake, I know it. I know that the percentage of criminals of our black fellow men is only slightly higher than the white percentage. I'm also aware that the blacks are recent immigrants and are learning to deal with a new environment, but I don't always practice my knowledge."

De Gier selected a fresh match. "You arrested the Prime Punk?"

"I did. He was breaking into a car. Karate caught him red-handed; the Punk was using a wonderbar. A wonderbar is a metal tool and he hit Karate with it. Karate thereupon attacked the Punk and I couldn't stop him in time. The Punk was in a bad state afterward. I admonished Karate for a few minutes and interrogated the Punk for an hour. I said that it was about time that we caught him and that I would make sure that he would receive the maximum punishment. I thereupon appealed to his sense of logic. I implored him to confess all his crimes so that he would only be punished once and not repeatedly. The Punk has never been arrested yet and we don't have his fingerprints. Knowing that he works without gloves, I told him that we found fingerprints on a silver-colored Mercedes with a Hamburg registration yesterday. I said that, if the fingerprints matched his, he would be in more trouble than he was now, but that he could improve his position by confessing right now."

Grijpstra no longer reclined in his chair. De Gier's match broke again, but he didn't take another.

"Ah," Sergeant Jurriaans said, "I see that I have your attention. Yes, my friends, it was him, him and an unidentified helper."

Grijpstra sighed. "He didn't kill Boronski. Our corpse

died of natural causes. We'll never break the doctor's statement. A large duodenal ulcer, no human hand. What did the Prime Punk say about Boronski?"

"He said that he and his helper, whose identity he can't remember, hot-wired the Mercedes in front of the Oberon and drove it to the Gentleman's Market. They parked the car and pried the trunk open. There was nothing in the trunk. They closed the lid and got back into the car, intending to go for a joy ride, when the trunk's lid popped open. Because they had forced the lid, it no longer closed easily. They got out to close it again, when a man came staggering along. It was around midnight and there was nobody else about."

"They didn't rob Boronski," Grijpstra said.

"No. They may have intended to, thinking the man would be drunk and helpless. As they approached Boronski, the man doubled up and vomited blood. He took a few more steps and held on to the trunk's lid. He fell into the trunk."

"As I thought," Grijpstra said. "As I thought all the time."

"Did he fall in altogether?" de Gier asked.

"No, but a patrol car passed on the other side of the canal. The constables in the car weren't paying attention, but the Prime Punk didn't want to be seen with a bleeding drunk. He expected the patrol car to come back on his side of the canal. He pushed Boronski into the trunk, slammed the lid, and walked away. He thought that the man would sleep in the trunk and that there would be enough air, because the lid didn't close properly. He expected the man to be found in the morning."

"Death by guilt," Grijpstra said. "You have a charge. The doctor said that Boronski could have been saved if he had been taken to hospital straightaway."

"The charge has already been laid. Now for the Prime Punk himself." He picked up his phone.

Within a minute the suspect was brought in. The young man's face was made up and his jacket carried a number of gaudy brooches, a bottle opener that had been unscrewed from a bar counter, a framed photograph of Alain Delon, and a German Iron Cross. His short hair was dyed with henna. His fingernails were painted orange. He didn't say anything. His jaw was bruised and his left ear bandaged.

"You can take him away again. Remove his ornamentation so that he can't hurt himself." The elderly constable accompanying the Prime Punk saluted.

"End of the case," Sergeant Jurriaans said when the door closed again. "I didn't mean to fish in your water, I just happened to be around when the fellow could be caught."

"Another cow catches another rabbit," de Gier said. "Here's money." He counted seven twenty-five guilder bills. "How much did you get, Grijpstra?"

Grijpstra put another seven bills on Jurriaans's desk.

"You're not paying me, are you?"

"No, we mugged two muggers. Black Jackets. They were in our way and if we hadn't acted serious, they might have hung about. You probably had a complaint at this station tonight. Somebody must have lost the 350 that the Black Jackets split among themselves. I hope it was only one robbery. If this is the total of several felonies, you may have complications."

Jurriaans laughed. "You must have shaken them. It so happens that I do have a complainant who lost that amount tonight, a parson from the provinces who happened to stray into one of the bad streets around here. Do you remember what your fellows looked like?"

"Perhaps this little matter shouldn't be pursued," Grijpstra said. "Just return the venerable sucker's money, will you?"

"I will," Jurriaans said and tucked the bills into an envelope which he licked carefully. "Perhaps the parson doesn't want to pursue the matter either. He's a married man and the street where he was caught has a prostitute behind every window." He looked at his watch. "Are you free now? I am, and I live close by; I can go home and change. We could meet at Beelema's."

Grijpstra got up. "No, I've been there twice already tonight, and it is a place I'm trying to avoid. We still have some work to do. Some other time, Jurriaans, at another café, and thank you."

"The pleasure is mine."

They met Karate at the door. He looked at Asta. "How're you doing?"

"She's fine," de Gier said.

"I'm not," Asta said. "My knee hurts and needs a compress. A wet towel will do. I should lie on a bed. Do you have a towel?"

"He'll have a bed too," Karate said.

De Gier turned on the small constable. "Just for that, you can drive us to Headquarters and pick up my bicycle on the way, and you can drive me home, too, after we're done."

Karate opened the side door of the minibus.

"Be my guest, sergeant."

Grijpstra sat in front. He pushed away the partitioning between the driver's compartment and the rear of the bus and tapped de Gier on the shoulder.

"Rinus?"

"Yes?"

"We have no murder."

De Gier smiled. "Are you sure?"

"No."

The bus drove off.

Asta's hand slid into the sergeant's. "You mean it isn't over yet?"

"No, but we'll have to start all over again and in a different way."

"Good," she said, "I need more time with you, and my knee hurts."

"I have a towel at home," de Gier said and looked at a window where a tall black woman in white lace underwear stared back at him. She smiled; the mauve neon lighting of the small room made her teeth light up. She pulled a hidden string and her bra opened for a moment, displaying a perfect bosom.

Asta's elbow hit the sergeant's chest.

"Uh."

"Did you like her?"

"So-so."

"Did you like me in the bath today?"

"Yes."

"Good," she said. "Let's not spend too much time on Herr Müller." She tapped on the partitioning and yelled at Karate. "Let's go!"

The minibus's faulty siren howled hesitantly, worn gears ground painfully, a profound rattle shook the vehicle. Karate, jaw set, bent down over the wheel and mumbled encouragingly; the car picked up some speed.

It stopped again for some drunks who tottered from sidewalk to sidewalk in the narrow street.

"Sorry," Karate said, "only civilians can speed in Amsterdam."

"Yes," Grijpstra said, "or no. Never mind. Maybe I see it now, but I don't see all of it."

"Beg pardon, adjutant?"

"A chaos."

"It sure is, adjutant. See that respectable lady over

there? With the hat in her eyes? A schoolmistress or a welfare worker. Drunk as a coot. How the hell did she fall into sin?"

"I've never accepted the chaos," Grijpstra said. "Perhaps I should. Turn up that siren, constable, we've got to get out of here."

8

"But look here," Grijpstra said, "you were seen opening your case, taking out a small plastic bag, and
pulling back your arm with the obvious intention of
throwing the bag into the canal. We subsequently
searched the case, which you closed again when you
were arrested and managed to kick into the water.
The case contained plastic bags, and each bag, according to our laboratory, was filled with a quarter of a
pound of first-class cocaine. All in all, you had four
pounds of high-priced junk in there. True or not?"

Müller's chins moved convulsively in a fluid movement upward until his thick lips trembled slightly.
Grijpstra wasn't sure how to interpret this facial agita-
tion. "Are you smiling, Herr Müller?"

"I am."

"Why?"

"Because you're wrong."

"You weren't about to throw the cocaine into the canal?"

The fat man's hands shifted slightly on his belly, which was pushed up obscenely and ready to flow over the edge of Grijpstra's desk.

"Your facts are correct but your explanation isn't. The case belonged to Boronski. He left it in my room; perhaps he planted the case on me, I don't know. Boronski was a sick man. He chose my car to die in; perhaps that desire was intentional too, again I don't know. We weren't getting on well; I was displeased with the quality of his shipments. I told him that I might find another supplier. He wasn't in his right mind, he was hallucinating, he was causing trouble in the hotel."

"Really?" Grijpstra asked. "So why would you destroy the cocaine, why didn't you give it to us?"

Müller's face appeared to become more solid. A crafty light flickered in his protruding eyes.

"Tell me, Herr Müller."

"Because you are the police. The police here are no good. The food is no good either. Nothing is good here."

There was a newspaper on Grijpstra's desk. The adjutant glanced at the headlines. *Further moves in drug scandal.* He had read the article earlier that day. The paper claimed that charges would be pressed against several highly placed police officers.

"Yes," Müller said. "I'm from Hamburg, our dialect is similar to Dutch. I can read your newspapers. What would happen if I gave you four pounds of cocaine?"

"It would be confiscated and in due time destroyed."

"Nein."

"Nein?"

"Nein. It would disappear. It would make you rich. I don't want to make you rich. Cocaine is bad. It would still reach the addicts. I decided to do some good work. I'm an honest merchant, I deal in lumber. My material goes into homes and furniture. I protect society. I took the risk to do away with the poison myself, but you prevented my service to society."

Grijpstra nodded pleasantly. "You could also have burned it, or flushed it down the toilet."

"I'm not a chemist. Perhaps cocaine explodes when it burns. Perhaps it does not dissolve easily. I did not want to clog up the hotel plumbing. I thought I was doing the right thing, but you interfered."

Grijpstra got up. "Fine. I will now take you back to your cell."

Müller got up too. "I want some cigarettes and matches."

"But of course. We will get them from the machine on our way to the cell block. By the way, Herr Müller, there's another charge against you. You resisted arrest and attacked an officer. You hurt her knee."

Müller smiled triumphantly.

"This way," Grijpstra said.

He came back a few minutes later, sat down, and dialed.

"No," a female voice said, "the teletyper is in use by your chief."

"My chief is at home."

"He's here."

"Here? Doing what?" Grijpstra looked at his watch. "It's two in the morning."

"He's using the teletyper."

Grijpstra looked at the telephone.

"Will that be all, adjutant?"

"No. Get me the Hamburg Police Headquarters, Inspector Wingel, drugs department. He won't be there, but they'll know where to find him. I'll wait here for his call."

"I don't speak German," the girl said.

"Then just get me the number."

It took twenty minutes before Wingel was on the phone. His voice sounded sleepy but became clipped when he understood what he was told. "Yes," he said. "Yes."

Grijpstra yawned. "I thought you might be interested."

"I am. I'll be right over."

"Here?"

"There. I'll leave now and bring a colleague. There won't be much traffic. We'll be there in three hours."

"Very well," Grijpstra said. "I'll wait for you." He let the telephone drop back on its hook. He yawned again. He picked up the phone again.

"Who is the commissaris talking to? Not to the German police, is he?"

"No, adjutant. To Colombia. It took us forever to make the connection. He's got himself set up in the other office. He's been there for more than an hour; he's speaking to our embassy out there."

Five minutes later the adjutant was asleep, his head against the wall, his feet on his desk. The remnants of a grin eased his face and he burbled placidly through pursed lips. De Gier was asleep, too, at the edge of his bed to give room to Tabriz who had stretched herself on a wet towel. She had come in late and nudged Asta's body aside patiently, pushing the girl with her nose and soft paws. Even Müller was asleep, snoring heavily while he fought shapeless fiends that tore at his lies. Boronski was dead, more dead than when the detectives observed his stiffening features. Perhaps his spirit was about, but the attendant Jacobs no longer cared. He had built his transparent insubstantial egg and sat within it, peacefully puffing on his battered pipe, studying a Hebrew text through his little round glasses.

Only the commissaris was awake, waiting for the teletyper to rattle again and reading through a stack of paper with torn edges that recorded his conversation so far.

9

The commissaris had gone home that afternoon and limped up the cracked cement steps to be embraced by his wife, stripped out of his clothes, and lowered into a hot bath. In his bath he was without pain, for his rheumatism was eased by the steam and the swirl of minute soapy waves, as well as the coffee, and the cigar that his wife brought and lit ceremoniously, before placing it carefully between his lips. She hovered about while he read the paper, skipping over the headlines and the editorial and concentrating on two items. Astronomers, an article tucked away into the far corner of an inside page told him, had discovered a new galaxy; it was about the size of the Milky Way and would, therefore, contain the same number of planets that were the size of the earth, at about the same distance from their suns, at more or less the same state of development; approximately a million. The commissaris chuckled. The other item informed him that a Gypsy child on the outskirts of the city died that morning. She had, somehow, fallen into burning rubbish. The identity of the child had not been established; she was about three years old.

"A new galaxy," the commissaris said to his wife. "At three billion inhabitants each, multiplied by one million. How much would that be?"

"I don't know, dear."

"Would their suffering add up to the fear and pain of one child?"

His wife did not hear him, she was letting a little more hot water into the bath. "Are you comfortable, dear?"

"Very."

"Afterward you should have a nap."

He slept, first thinking, then dreaming about Boronski. After a while, he was conscious of waking up but resisted and slipped into no man's land where everything is instantaneously possible and solutions rise up like bubbles, each holding a complete picture.

He dressed and left. His wife accompanied him to the front door.

"You won't work, will you?"

"A little."

"In your office?"

"Oh yes."

His sleek Citroën was respectfully greeted by the old constable in charge of the large courtyard behind Headquarters. He reacted by lifting a finger. He didn't see the old man, he didn't see anybody in the corridors either. In the teletype room he asked to be connected to the Dutch embassy in Bogotá, Colombia. After a good while the machine came to life. He heard the staccato of the keys, saw the words form.

"Please go ahead."

He gave his name and rank and asked for the ambassador.

"He's lunching."

"This is urgent. Please find him."

"It'll take time. He's not in the building. There are some festivities. Perhaps later in the afternoon . . ."

"It's late evening here, the matter cannot wait."

"Yes sir. You'll hear from us."

The commissaris returned to his room and brought out his projector. He unrolled the screen and closed the curtains. He sat and gazed at the slide showing Boronski and the unknown woman. The telephone rang two hours later; he was asked to return to the teletype room.

"This is the ambassador."

"Do you know a man by the name of Jim Boronski?"

"Yes."

"He died here in Amsterdam yesterday. There are some complications. Please describe the man to me, not his body, his mind, please."

The machine hummed. A minute passed.

"Are you there?"

"Yes," the machine wrote, "but remember that I'm a diplomat. I've also consumed a fair quantity of alcohol. This is not the time to make an official statement that is recorded at your and my end."

"Are you dictating this message?"

"I am."

"Can you handle the teletyper yourself?"

"I suppose so."

"Please make direct contact with me. I will ask the lady who's assisting me to leave this room and will write myself. Afterward I will destroy the messages."

The commissaris nodded at the female constable sitting next to him. She got up and left the room.

The machine hesitated. "This is . . ."

"Go ahead."

"The ambassador. Are you alone?"

"I am."

"What's your age?"

"Sixty-three."

"What is your job?"

"Chief of the murder brigade."

"Will you give me some private advice?"

The commissaris sat back. He reread the sentence, then reached for the keys. "Yes."

"I'm in personal trouble. I'm also drunk. The lunch was heavy. I need advice; do I have your word of honor that this correspondence will be destroyed?"

"Yes."

"I'm fifty years old. I'm partly homosexual. I'm married and have children, not yet grown up. My family does not know about my sexual inclinations. I appear to be normal."

"Homosexuality is not abnormal," the commissaris typed slowly.

"So I hear. I don't believe it. I'm ashamed. You understand?"

"Yes."

"I have a lover. A Colombian. Sometimes I visit him. He has had us photographed."

"I see."

"The photographs are revolting."

"So you say."

"I could describe them to you. You would agree then."

"I would not."

"Are you homosexual?"

"No."

"Are you faithful to your wife?"

"Lately yes; I'm old and suffer advanced rheumatism."

"And before?"

"Yes, I was unfaithful."

"Often?"

"There were certain bursts of activity."

"Were you ever blackmailed?"

"No, but it has been tried."

"Photographs?"

"No, correspondence."

"What did you do?"

"I told the lady to go ahead. She did. Photocopies of what I wrote were sent to my wife and my chief."

"What happened?"

"I had some trouble, not too much, the truth is the best lie."

"My trouble is more serious than yours was."

"I don't agree."

The machine hummed for nearly two minutes. The commissaris lit a cigar. He puffed and watched the paper in the machine.

"You know, Colombia is not The Netherlands. Guns are for hire here. My enemy is evil. I was set up. He'll go to the limit."

"Don't."

"The matter could be arranged, I know where to go. A colleague was in the same predicament. His problem was taken care of."

"Don't."

"What if there's a scandal? I will lose my job, my wife, my children. At my age I cannot find other employment, I'll rot somewhere in fear, in misery. I'll be alone."

"You won't, but even so, there is always something worthwhile to do. Murder is a lowly way out and will twist back on you."

The reply was prompt. "Yes." There was a pause. "What would you do in my case?"

The commissaris put his cigar on the edge of the machine. He typed slowly and carefully. "I would sit in my garden and communicate with my friend. Do you have a garden?"

"Yes. Who is your friend?"

"My friend is a turtle."

The machine was quiet.

"You're laughing, aren't you?" the commissaris asked.

"I am. Your advice is good. I have a small dog, I will communicate with him tomorrow morning when I'm sober."

"What sort of dog?"

"Small, white with black spots, ugly. I found him a year ago, starving, covered with vermin."

"He'll confirm my advice."

"Yes."

"Boronski?" the commissaris asked.

The machine picked up speed.

"No good. I know him fairly well. An amoral small-time tycoon. Deals in lumber and anything else that is profitable. Smuggles whisky into the country, on a fairly large scale. Probably exports drugs. Owns a large villa in the suburbs. Originally a ship's steward, worked his way up rapidly. Goes to most of the parties of the foreign community to show off his importance. Unmarried, but attractive to women. There have been unsavory affairs."

"How unsavory?"

"He uses women, then drops them when he feels bothered or as soon as they bore him. There have been divorces and at least one suicide."

The commissaris closed his eyes, opened them again, and typed out a description of the woman in the photograph. "Is she known to you?"

"Yes. She doesn't live here, she came on a South

American vacation with her husband. They were due to go to Rio from here, but she stayed behind to continue her affair with Boronski."

"For long?"

"No. Boronski tired of her, he has a lot of choice here. She had no money and came to the embassy for help. We contacted her husband who paid for her ticket. About two months ago. She fell down the stairs in her hotel, slipped a disc and left in a wheelchair."

"Her name?"

"I forget, I'll phone my wife. Hold on."

The commissaris stretched.

"I have her name. Marian Hyme. Her husband works for a publishing company in Amsterdam. Was Boronski killed?"

"Yes."

"How?"

"He was harassed to death."

"Will you be able to prove that?"

"No."

"So why bother?"

The commissaris lit another cigar. He smoked peacefully.

"I see," the machine wrote. "Thank you for your advice. I trust you. Goodbye."

"Goodbye."

The commissaris got up and tore the sheet out of the teletyper. He crumpled it, together with the others that had slipped off the small table attached to the machine. He dropped the paper into a metal waste-paper basket, held the container on its side, and lit a match. The paper burned fiercely and the smoke hurt his eyes, but he held on until the flaming balls fell apart into black crisp shreds. He stirred the ashes with a ruler. Two girls came into the room.

"Is there a fire? Are you all right, sir?"

He coughed. "Yes. I'm sorry I made a mess. I threw a burning match into the trash can, silly habit of mine. My wife keeps warning me and I keep on doing it." He left the room while the constables opened windows and waved the smoke away with a plastic tablecloth.

It was quiet in the building as he walked to the corridor to take the elevator back to his office. He found Grijpstra and two middle-aged men waiting near his door.

"Sir," Grijpstra said, "I'm glad to see you. These gentlemen are Inspector Wingel and Subinspector Roider of the Hamburg Police. I have interrogated the suspect Müller, without success so far. These colleagues now request permission to speak with him. They have met him before and are interested to find out what connections he may have in Germany."

The two men straightened up and clacked their heels as the commissaris shook their hands.

"Why not? We're always happy to oblige."

Grijpstra smiled apologetically. "They want to see him right away, sir. They say it's better when the suspect is tired. We arrested Müller tonight because he was in possession of four pounds of high-grade cocaine and because he kicked and hurt Constable Asta's knee. She was in pain."

The commissaris stiffened. "She was, was she? How is she now?"

"De Gier took care of her, sir. They left together earlier on."

"Nothing serious?"

"Not too serious."

The commissaris looked into the cold eyes of the German inspector. "You may go ahead; my adjutant will find you a suitable office. Do you have a hotel?"

"We'll find a hotel later, Herr Kommissar, we know our way about in Amsterdam." Wingel bowed stiffly.

The commissaris watched the three men walk away, Grijpstra leisurely ahead, the German policemen marching slowly in step. He shuddered and his hand missed the door handle of his room.

10

"Good," the commissaris said while he read through the large menu, handwritten on elegant paper. "A new restaurant, but obviously handled by the right people. Even the chief constable recommends it. Hmmm, oysters. Hmmm, mushrooms. Hmmm, sirloin steak. Yes. Well, have you all made up your mind? I'm sorry I'm late, but I couldn't find a parking place easily and I've forgotten my cane, took a while to get here. Oysters, Grijpstra?"

The waiter took his time writing down the order and the commissaris sipped his drink. Asta sat opposite him.

"How's your knee, dear?"

"The swelling is going down, sir."

"I trust you had a restful night?"

Asta looked at de Gier. "Not quite. The sergeant has a cat. I woke up in the middle of the night because I thought my alarm went off." She pointed at an electronic watch that seemed far too large for her slim wrist. "I switched it off, but the beeping went on. It was the cat and a friend."

"The cat beeped?"

"No sir. The friend. A mouse. I suppose Tabriz wanted to catch the mouse, but the mouse didn't want to play. It got annoyed. When I switched on the light, I saw the mouse jumping, a foot high, right in front of the cat. Every time the mouse faced Tabriz, it beeped. It was a rhythmical sound, that's why I thought my alarm went off."

"I'll have another drink," the commissaris said, holding up his glass. "I see. These are modern times indeed. Not only do you spend the night with a lover, you're telling us about it."

"He didn't love me, sir. My knee still hurt. I didn't want to go home. My landlady doesn't approve of latecomers and I don't have a key for the night lock. There was no choice."

The commissaris offered de Gier a match. "Sergeant?"

"Yes sir. Thank you, sir."

"You'll never learn, will you? Is there a happy end to the tale?"

"Yes sir. She made me get up and take the mouse down to the park. It wasn't hurt. Tabriz couldn't go to sleep after that; she rattled about in the kitchen. Kept me awake."

The meal was served and the commissaris was the first to finish his plate. He sat back and lit a cigar. "The chief constable was right, this is an excellent place to have lunch. Now then, I must congratulate you three on the arrest of Müller. I would like to hear the details. Tell me, adjutant, but eat your potato first."

Grijpstra reported. The salt cellar became Müller

a toothpick was Asta, the Black Jackets turned into two black olives, de Gier was a small cigar, and Grijpstra himself the pepper shaker.

"No," the commissaris said, "you mean to say that you mugged the robbers?"

"There was no other way, sir. We had to keep them away from Asta. We couldn't arrest them because they hadn't done anything yet. If we'd merely stopped them, they might have shouted or interfered with Müller's arrest in some other way."

The commissaris pushed his spectacles to his forehead. He picked up the olives and ate them, then he chuckled. "Hee hee, Grijpstra."

"I'm sorry, sir, but we did a good thing; the parson got his money back."

"Hee hee." The commissaris laughed helplessly. Two tears streamed down his cheeks. He wiped them away with his handkerchief. "How silly, Grijpstra, how *apt*. What splendid fellows you two sometimes are."

"And Müller confessed, sir," de Gier said. "We got his statement this morning in German. Inspector Wingel gave it to us, signed and witnessed by himself and his assistant."

The commissaris was serious again; he blew on his spectacles and wiped them carefully. "Yes? I thought Müller wasn't too cooperative after the arrest."

"He wasn't," Grijpstra said, "but he weakened when the German inspector woke him up somewhat roughly, sir. They had him for two hours after that."

"Were you there?"

"No sir, I waited in my office. They interrogated him in a room on another floor. It was five in the morning then and there wasn't anybody in the building, except the staff of the radio room. I thought I heard Müller scream a few times. When I saw him again, there was a stream of spittle running out of the side of his mouth and he seemed dazed. Subinspector Roider had gloves on; he was taking them off when he escorted the suspect to my office. Müller's face seemed abnormally red."

"Ah."

"The German colleagues were pleased, sir. The suspect had provided them with some names and addresses in Hamburg and other cities. He also made a full confession. Apparently Boronski had brought down the first consignment of cocaine to get the connection started. Future deliveries would be made by couriers, so-called tourists, nice elderly couples who would have their trips paid for and receive an ample fee on top of expenses. This was the first time Müller bought drugs from Boronski. Until now their business was legitimate."

"Where did he buy before?"

"From Turkey through Lebanon and France, but that traffic was stopped by the French police a while back. He was buying heroin then, but cocaine is about as profitable."

"Have the Germans left?"

"Yes. They said Müller was lucky that he was caught here and not in his own country. The penalties in Germany are stiffer, here he'll only get a few years."

"True," the commissaris said. "Did you ask him anything about Boronski's death?"

"Yes, he denies having anything to do with that."

"Do you believe him?"

"Yes sir." Grijpstra was playing with the menu that the waiter had replaced next to the commissaris's plate.

"Yes," the commissaris said, "we'll choose our desserts in a minute. Why don't you believe that Müller killed Boronski?"

Grijpstra put the menu down and held up two fingers. "First, Boronski was Müller's goose that lays the golden eggs. Second, Müller wouldn't have placed the body in his own car, a car reportedly stolen at the time and looked for by the police."

De Gier held up a finger too. "Boronski died of an ulcer, sir."

They ordered and ate their desserts. It took a while, for both Grijpstra and Asta selected the special, which came in a tall glass and had many layers of different ice creams, topped with fruit and whipped cream.

"Boronski was killed," the commissaris said when Asta licked her spoon. "He was attacked by a mind that was more subtle and agile than his own, and manipulated to the point where his fear and uncertainty turned inward and gnawed through his gut. Remember Mr. Fortune, this case is similar. Fortune faltered, became accident prone, fell afoul of the police, and was dumped into the Brewerscanal. But there was some insight in him and he managed to save himself. Fear eventually strengthened Fortune; it destroyed Boronski, understandably, I suppose. Boronski was, I hear, rather a rotter, and Fortune, according to your reports, seems to be a nice fellow."

De Gier deposited the remnants of a match into the ashtray. "Is good stronger than evil, sir?"

"I've often wondered about that," the commissaris said, "and I do believe that I have had some indications that the supposition may be true. The subject is tricky, sergeant. Good is useful and evil destroys. Sometimes it is good to destroy, and useful is often a shallow definition; it's relative, of course." He folded his napkin. "If we imagine that a drug dealer is a bad man and that a publisher ready to retire in solitude to meditate on the center of things is a good man, and if we bring them both into stress situations by playing about with their environment, and if they are both of the same strength, I would say that Boronski will go under and Fortune will come out on top. But the experiment starts at the end and I've built up its base afterward. We know that Fortune is a happy man today and Boronski's spirit is in hell, if I'm to believe Mr. Jacobs, the morgue attendant."

"You seem to have investigated Boronski's death further, sir."

The commissaris wrote a check. He looked up. "I have, Grijpstra. I spoke to an acquaintance of the dead man last night by teletype. The lady in the photograph you studied in my office yesterday is a Marian Hyme, the wife of a local publisher."

"Hyme," Grijpstra said.

"The name is familiar?"

"Back to Beelema, sir. It's the last place I want to go to. I was there twice yesterday. I can't get away from it."

"Tell me what you know about Mr. Hyme," the commissaris said, "and I'll tell you what I know. If we pool our ignorance, Mr. Hyme may turn out to be our missing link."

11

"I must ask you to calm down," the commissaris said. "Please sit down, sir, and don't shout."

Hyme sat down. His pale face framed a flabby and twitching mouth. "Boronski! The bastard! Dropped Marian like a sack of potatoes when he was through with her. Destroyed her dignity. She was a beautiful woman, intelligent, witty. You should see her now. *He* saw her. He came to the hospital to see if she was about to get out. Looking for a free fuck. Man hasn't been in Amsterdam for years and he has no connections here. He let her go in Bogotá, pushed her out of his palace with hardly enough time to pack her suitcase, but here he comes running after her. Marian has just been operated on again; she's flat on her back and in pain. It's the second operation and they don't know yet if they got the disc back in place this time. If it's where it should be, it'll be another six months before she can walk. When Boronski realized there was nothing doing, he shook her hand and left. I'm surprised he didn't take his flowers with him; he could have given them to somebody else. He had wasted his money."

"So you were aware that Boronski was in Amsterdam. Did you meet him at the hospital?"

"No. Marian told me about his visit."

"Did you meet with him here?"

"Briefly, on the Brewerscanal. I ran into him; he stays at Hotel Oberon. When I met him, I couldn't speak. The man has ruined my life. That vacation to South America was the worst hell I've ever lived through. We were invited to a cocktail party at the embassy and Marian fell for the bastard immediately. I thought it was a little flirtation, but she went home with him. She checked out of the hotel. We had a terrible scene; everything was said, everything that has ever been bad between us. I thought it would be the ultimate farewell, but she came back to me. She probably still loves him."

Hyme hid his face in his hands. Grijpstra sucked patiently on his cigar. De Gier studied a stain on the wall.

"Would you like some coffee?"

"Yes."

De Gier poured the coffee. The cup rattled on its saucer when Hyme took it.

"Did you see Boronski at his hotel, Mr. Hyme?"

"No. If I had, I would have killed him. I'm not a violent man, but I must have changed. I keep on thinking of ways to destroy that devil. I thought of having him kidnapped, locking him up in some dungeon, torturing him, but what can I do? The days a man could take revenge are over. I'm not too courageous anyway, that's why Marian got bored with me. I'm a slave, chained to my desk. My only act of bravery is pissing off bridges and I can only do that when I'm drunk."

"Yes," Grijpstra said softly.

"With a paper hat on. I'm the knight of the paper hat and the wooden sword, riding a rocking horse."

"Ah," the commissaris said. "What sort of a car do you have, Mr. Hyme."

"What?"

"What sort of a car do you drive?"

"A Porsche."

"With the wheel on the right side?"

"How do you know?"

"I guessed."

Hyme drank his coffee. The room was quiet. Grijpstra got up and left. The telephone on the commissaris's desk rang.

"Yes?"

"It's me, sir, Grijpstra. Can I have a word with you in the corridor?"

"Yes?" the commissaris asked when he had closed the door behind him.

"We might as well arrest him, don't you think, sir? The car checks out, he had the opportunity and the motive. He must have paid the employees of the Oberon to play tricks on Boronski."

"You can arrest him, adjutant."

Grijpstra reached for the door handle, but the small almost transparent hand of the commissaris rested lightly on his sleeve.

"I wouldn't advise you to do that, however. Harassment is difficult to prove and hardly punishable. You'll find yourself wasting endless time in a court case where the lawyers will have a field day. Besides, Hyme is not your man."

Grijpstra stepped away from the door. "He isn't?"

"No. I admit that the suspect's nerves are in a bad

state and that he may be at the lowest point of his life.
But you mustn't forget that he is a director of a large
and successful firm. Mr. Hyme is no fool. He's not
a genius either. Only a genius would have confirmed,
in the way he just did, that his dearest wish is to do
away with Boronski, and tried to prove his innocence
in such a perverse way."

"Shall we tell him that Boronski is dead, sir?"

"We can do that now."

"Dead?" whispered Hyme. "When?"

"Yesterday. Jim Boronski bled to death internally.
A severe duodenal ulcer. Some would-be muggers saw
him staggering about on the Gentleman's Market just
after midnight on Saturday and, for some reason,
dumped him in the trunk of a car. He must have died
shortly afterward."

"My God," Hyme said. "But he was still a young
man."

"Young men die too, Mr. Hyme. Your enemy must
have labored under heavy stress. He suffered, but
didn't go to a doctor. His complaint worsened, circumstances were against him, and . . ." The commissaris gestured.

"Dead," Hyme said.

"Where were you last night, sir?"

"I ate in a restaurant, visited Marian at the hospital,
went home, and watched TV."

"And the night before, Sunday evening."

"Same thing."

"You weren't at Café Beelema last night?"

"No."

"And the night before?"

"No. I was there Saturday and met with your assistants."

Grijpstra raised a hand. "Have you met with Mr. Fortune recently?"

"Yes, yesterday. We arranged for the take-over of his firm. He came to my office. I was glad to hear that his wife turned up after all."

"Did Mr. Fortune tell you about Boronski's death?"

"Frits Fortune? No. Why should he? He doesn't even know Boronski."

"Did Borry Beelema know Boronski?" de Gier asked.

"Yes. I pointed him out to Beelema. Hotel Oberon is just across the street from Beelema's."

"When was that?"

"Last week some time."

"Did you confide in Beelema about your troubles with Boronski?"

Hyme nodded. "Yes. Beelema is a friend. I've known him for years, ever since he bought the café. Before that I was his client at the hair salon, I still go there every fortnight and at the café I see him several times a week. He's my best friend." He smiled. "He's more than a friend, he's an incarnate angel. A lot of people call him the other son of God."

"Did you," de Gier asked, "by any chance, some time last week, lend your . . ."

The commissaris jumped up with such force that his chair hit the wall.

"That'll be all, Mr. Hyme. Thank you for coming here. I hope your wife's condition will soon improve. Adjutant, please escort Mr. Hyme out of the building."

12

"This is the best time of the day," Beelema said. "They've all just got home and there'll be dinner in a minute. The town is quiet. The town is so much more beautiful when there's no bustle, don't you think? Like one of those old prints or glass paintings—they only show the buildings and the water, maybe a boat moored to a tree. People are a nuisance."

"Indeed," the commissaris said. He was leaning over the railing watching a duck. The duck's head was submerged, and it was waving its bright orange feet. A litle farther down a swan floated, asleep, its feathers precisely arranged. It bobbed almost imperceptibly on the slow ripple of the canal's weak current.

"It was good of you to come to see me. You're not here professionally, I understand?"

"Oh yes," the commissaris said, "I'm here professionally but not officially. You've committed a crime, but I won't arrest you if that's what you're getting at. My curiosity has brought me; I would like to know the details of what you managed to bring about."

Beelema unclipped a gold toothpick off the chain that spanned his ample stomach and pressed it slowly between his teeth. He took it out and spat. The duck retrieved its head, quacked, and paddled away; the swan looked up sleepily and reinserted its beak between its backfeathers. "But perhaps you could arrest me. Some of my deeds could be proved, I suppose; you might get some sort of case together."

"No. The law we uphold is primitive. I would have to prove intent to kill. Did you intend to kill Boronski?"

Beelema fumbled with the toothpick. Its clip was small and he had to bring out his spectacles to finish the operation. "No, not really, but he died."

"You see, there goes one charge. Yet you killed the man as surely as if you had fired a bullet through his head. Death caused by guilt would be the better charge, but you would have to confess and I would have to produce witnesses who heard you state your intention to bother Boronski."

Beelema's fluffy white curls danced as he shook his head. "I wouldn't confess, and I told nobody, not even Hyme. The favor was a secret."

"Favor," the commissaris said softly.

Beelema smiled, and his golden canines caught the sunlight. "Yes, a favor to a friend. Hyme was harmed and couldn't defend himself. I have a talent; I'm imaginative and energetic. I'm also efficient. But I've reached all my goals. My hair salon is successful, I can live on it in luxury. The café goes well. I have all I want and to spare. I've no need for a car or a boat or an airplane or all the other gadgets rich people go in for. This area is all I care for, I hardly ever move outside it. When I found that I could help people unobtrusively, by pushing factors a little, by fitting parts into a whole, I began to experiment. I've been amazed at what I can do."

"Just amazed? Never frightened?"

"Never frightened. I listen to my friends, I observe them, I see what goes wrong with them, I also see ways to right the wrong. Sometimes I concentrate when I sit at the bar or walk about in my shop or stand on this bridge, but often the thoughts just pop into my head. You've seen two examples of my work. I liberated Frits Fortune and I balanced the scales in Hyme's head. There have been other examples that I won't mention because I'm not trying to impress you. I didn't ask for my talent. It just came to me to be used."

The commissaris was watching a sparrow now, investigating ripening seeds on a weed growing between stones. "Ah."

"You don't approve? You must be doing the same thing, or do you wait until there's a deadlock and the man goes down? Do you kick him when he is down? I've often wondered about the police. In a way I also police this area; I restore order."

The commissaris smiled. "We usually wait until it's too late. *Optima civi cives.* The highest value of a citizen is the citizenry. We'll let them muddle through as best they can and only interfere when they break the law."

"When it's too late."

The commissaris nodded. "When they break the law, it is too late. But they shouldn't break the law."

"Pfff."

"I beg your pardon?"

Beelema turned and found the right place for the railing to support his back. He was of the same size as the commissaris but nearly twice as wide.

"The law. Rules and regulations, I never liked them. As a toddler I took part in a school performance; I had to dance with the other kids in a circle. I kept on leaving the circle and dancing the other way. I don't remember that event, my mother told me about it. She was embarrassed. Everybody laughed and I wasn't allowed to finish the act. I see what goes wrong and I help others to find an original solution, contrary to custom. Fortune was unhappy, he'll be better off in his present position. Hyme was a wreck. He was turning into an alcoholic, swilling beer at my café, making a spectacle of himself on this bridge. Now he can face the world again. Boronski was a scoundrel; he didn't concern me until he crossed Hyme's path and therefore mine. I enjoyed that little game."

"Who was the lady who upset Boronski at Hotel Oberon?"

"Guess."

"Titania?"

"Never," Beelema said, poking the commissaris playfully in the side. "You don't know Titania, so you are excused. She can only perform when I'm right behind her. No, Rea Fortune, of course. She used to be an actress, not a very good one, I think, but good enough for this little drama. I mentioned the matter to her and she accepted immediately. Every woman is half a whore, Shakespeare said. She enjoyed being picked up by Boronski and went to the hotel with him. Sexually she is very capable. He had such a good time that he arranged for her to spend the night with him too at a stiff price, which he paid in advance. Even smart businessmen can be suckers. Rea used the cash to pay her expenses when she ran away from her husband." Beelema giggled. "Wonderful how it all fits together, don't you think? And she'll never breathe a word. She is with Zhaver now and Frits Fortune is going to give her a lot of money. Zhaver wants to open up on his own farther along, a small restaurant, I found it for him. There should always be change. He worked well for me, but it's time to replace him. I've already replaced Titania, too. How do you like the new girl?"

"Beautiful," the commissaris said.

"I've always liked black women. I'm having some white jumpsuits made for her. It'll be fun experimenting with how far the zipper should be pulled down. She has perfect breasts, but they shouldn't be exposed completely, I think."

The commissaris agreed.

"I'll ask the adjutant and that handsome sergeant to be on the committee. They're good men; they have the talent, too, I think. I sometimes recognize it in others. Not too often, though; it must be rare. *You* have it."

"Do I really?" The sparrow flew off. The commissaris turned his back to the railing too. "And the car? How did you arrange that? Hyme didn't know, did he? My sergeant was going to ask him, but I cut the question off. I didn't want Hyme to run to you and prevent this conversation or alter it."

Beelema burped. "Excuse me. Too rich a meal again. It'll be worse when Zhaver opens his restaurant. I should really go on a diet. Hyme? No, he never knew. He has a habit of leaving his car keys on the counter, and that night he had a lot to drink. I slipped out and got the two kitchen boys at Hotel Oberon to help me push Boronski's Porsche away. Then I replaced it with Hyme's Porsche and took all the stuff that Boronski had in his car and rearranged it carefully in Hyme's. The kitchen boys changed the number plates. When I knew that Boronski had seen the car, I changed everything back to normal again. No, Hyme never knew.

His Porsche was back where it had been by the time he went home."

"The kitchen boys also arranged the matter of the watch and the laundry?"

Beelema laughed. "You heard about that too? Yes. They were foreign students who have meanwhile left the country. They'll be hard to trace. They helped me with all the other set-ups too. Little things mostly. It's amazing how a man can be shaken by little things. I noticed that a long time ago at school, when I practiced on the teachers. It seems as if each man creates a foundation for himself, a pattern of habits. A teacher I particularly disliked would always hang his hat on a certain hook. I would take it off and hang it on the next hook. It drove him frantic. Nobody could understand why he got so upset. I sat in the hotel lounge sometimes and observed Boronski. I read some of his thoughts, analyzed his mind. He was neat. I arranged that the waitresses would spill on him, just a little, a drop of coffee, a tiny splash of ketchup. Can happen to anybody, they would apologize and pretend to clean his trousers or jacket and then they would worsen the stain somehow; women are very clever at that. There were other instances. I know the traffic attendant who writes out the parking tickets here; he drinks at my café. Boronski got a lot of tickets. My friend would wait for Boronski to come out of the hotel and make him pay in cash. And my dear old lady friend, Mrs. Cabbage-Tonto, pretended that Boronski had stepped on her Chihuahua and made a terrible scene in the street. Much more happened, I won't bore you with it all, but I had Boronski jumping during every waking minute, and I daresay I got into his dreams too."

"True," the commissaris said, "we live in patterns. We make them ourselves, they're our safety, and you dare to interfere with the patterns of others."

"With reason," Beelema said. "I'm entitled to do it; I have both the talent and the right. You don't agree?"

"No," the commissaris said.

"You don't," Beelema said. "I'm sorry to hear it. I thought you would agree. I've studied you a little. I took you for a superior man, like myself. But you're small-minded. You would be, of course, in your official capacity, but I thought you would liberate yourself from prejudice in your spare time. However, no matter, would you care to step into my café and have a drink with me?"

"I would not," the commissaris said, "but I thank you for satisfying my curiosity."

Beelema did not move.

"Is that your last word? I had hoped for a little more."

"There is the law," the commissaris whispered so that Beelema had to lean over to hear him. "I don't mean the law in our books, that's no more than a projection. The true law is in all of us, in our center, in the core of our being, where we are all connected and where the illusion of identity no longer obscures our insight. If you have, as you say, the talent, you are misusing it. Reflect, sir, and take care."

13

Summer changed into autumn, the heavy rains had passed, and the air was crisp. It was late at night and Beelema walked by himself. Kiran wasn't with him. The dog had refused to leave the house and snarled when Beelema tried to pet him. The dog's behavior had been gradually changing; he no longer bothered people and seemed tired and listless. The veterinarian could find nothing wrong with the Great Dane. Beelema worried about the dog. If Kiran continued to snarl at him, he might have to get rid of his pet.

Beelema also worried about himself. He was getting fatter. He also drank too much. He had been drinking a lot that particular evening, served by the two lovely barmaids, one black, one Indonesian. Yet everything was going well. The bar was crowded every evening and Zhaver's restaurant, in which he had an interest, was usually booked days in advance. He was busy in his hair salon too.

It's the time of the year, he thought, as he walked on, maneuvering around a corner and bumping his shoulder. It's autumn, nature is dying, the general decline affects me.

He bumped into a tree, softly, for his stomach protected him. Then he stumbled over a low fence. Really, Beelema thought, I must watch myself. I know every square inch of the area. This is where they keep blacktopping the same hole. Every time, it caves in again, and they bring out the machinery and make a new mess. He stepped back and walked around the fence.

A young man, a boy still, but tall and slender, walked toward the stumbling figure.

I still feel sexy, Beelema thought, that's good.

"You're a dear boy," he said aloud. "You're handsome. Walk with me a little way. We'll like each other."

The boy stopped. Beelema caressed his black leather jacket.

"Can I feel your skull? I like bare skulls. I shouldn't because I'm a hairdresser and naughty boys like you spoil my trade. You *are* naughty, aren't you?"

"Sure," the boy said. His teeth shone in a black regularly shaped face. Beelema's fat finger pressed on the aquiline nose.

"Yes, you are beautiful. Would you like some money? First we play together and then I give you some money. How much would you like, naughty boy?"

"He'll want all of your money," a voice said behind Beelema. Beelema tried to turn around but his shoulders were held.

"Let's take his gold too," the first boy said, "everything. He's got some in his mouth. Break it open and I'll knock it out. Use your knife."

"No," Beelema yelled, but his cry was cut short by a hand clasping his mouth. Another hand yanked off his watch chain. There seemed to be many hands, punching him, slapping his face, tugging at the rings on his fingers, removing his wallet, even the loose change from his pocket. The hands hurt him; there were hard feet too that kicked his ankles and shins. Then he felt a sharp pain in his neck.

"Don't say a word, sugar daddy, this is a sharp knife, it'll cut you and you'll bleed like a pig; you ever see a pig bleed?"

"Let's get his teeth," the first boy said.

"Hold him, I'll get my pliers. They're in the car. Don't run away now, sugar daddy, I'll be right back to take your nice teeth."

"And his nice balls," the first boy said. "He has gold balls too, haven't you, sugar daddy?"

Beelema pulled himself free. The boys allowed him to get away a few steps, then ran after him and pushed him down.

He fell on the fence, knocking it over, and rolled in the tar. The boys removed the top of the fence and pushed him so that he rolled on. He rolled till the tarmac was solid again, scrambled to his feet, and ran on. The boys were close behind, running soundlessly on their rubber-soled halfboots.

"Here," the first boy said.

A hand came down on Beelema's neck. He fell. There was the smell of blood.

"Bah, he's sticky. Give me that two-by-four. We'll roll him through that heap of feathers, maybe we can change him into a bird."

Beelema felt the hard edges of the stick and turned over to get away from it. Then there was nothing for a while. He woke because a light shone into his face.

"What do we have here, Ketchup?"

"Good question, Karate. A ball of feathers with eyes. What are you, sir?"

Beelema crawled away to escape the harsh light.

"Hey, stay here. What happened to you?"

The two policemen stared at each other. "What do we do now? Can't leave him. He's bleeding too."

"Ambulance," Karate said. "They'll fix him up at the hospital. Are you drunk, sir?"

Beelema tried to speak but coughed instead.

The ambulance arrived, but the attendants refused to lift him up. They found a plastic sheet and folded it so that it covered the stretcher.

"You take him in, you found him. It's the least you can do."

Karate went back to the fence and kicked until a thick board snapped free. He stuck the board between Beelema's legs and Ketchup held the other side. They lifted together.

"Right," the attendant said. "Easy now, don't drop him. Get him on the plastic. Yagh, what a mess."

"There you go, sir," Karate said. "We'll see you at the hospital."

14

The commissaris sat next to the bed. He held Bee-lema's hand. De Gier stood at the foot of the bed and agreed. The procedure was proper: always hold the victim's hand. That way he doesn't feel alone. Death is an agony that can be shared, up to a point of course. From there on, the victim is on his own again.

"Is he conscious?" the commissaris asked.

A young man in a white coat bent down.

"Barely."

"What is he dying of?"

"Can't say. The wounds don't appear to be too seri-ous, maybe the tar has interfered with his breathing. I thought we got most of it, but he may have been in that condition for hours. In some places we scraped off more than an inch and we had to use solvents to get rid of the rest. There's a bruise on the head, that may explain his predicament too. And there's fear. People can die of fright. A number of causes, I would say."

"This is the worst mugging I've ever seen," Grijpstra said. "They went all out."

The doctor felt Beelema's pulse and shook his head. "He's out too," the doctor said. "We'll have an autopsy to determine the exact nature of his death. I'll let you know what we come up with."

The commissaris released Beelema's hand. He got up and bowed his head.

"You warned him, didn't you, sir?" de Gier asked as he slid behind the wheel of the Citroën.

"Yes. But I was too late."

"We're always too late," Grijpstra said from the rear of the car.

The Citroën found a place in the heavy morning traffic and coasted slowly back to Headquarters. The commissaris led the way to the canteen.

"Too late," he said to de Gier, "but I think he was entitled to this, it was his right."

"Man has no rights," Grijpstra said, joining the line for the coffee machine, "only duties."

The commissaris held up his mug. "We have one right, adjutant, the right to face the consequences of our deeds."

De Gier mumbled as he shuffled through the crowd of constables and detectives, carrying a plate of apple cake and his coffee.

"What was that, sergeant?"

"What a way to go, sir. A nightmare. And it started out so well. Grijpstra danced and sang. I saw bits of beauty everywhere. We were floating right on top of the whole thing and then we got sucked in again."

The commissaris walked over to the cigarette machine, dropped in some coins and came back.

"It's all in your own mind, sergeant."

De Gier tore the pack open, took out a cigarette, accepted a light from Grijpstra, and sucked in the smoke.

"There," the adjutant said, "you'll feel better."

"Much."

"Everything is all right. Asta will be waiting for you when you come. She is a beautiful girl and she loves you."

"Yes."

"Security will be restored."

"Yes."

The commissaris touched de Gier's hand. "Security is in the mind too, Rinus."

The adjutant got up to reach over to the next table for some sugar. A passing constable didn't notice him and took his chair. When the adjutant tried to sit down again, he fell to the floor.

"I see." De Gier helped Grijpstra to his feet.

"I hope you haven't hurt yourself," the commissaris said and pulled up another chair.

In the wake of violent crime, from clue to clue, from puzzle to solution — come two of modern mystery's most clever and relentless sleuths—Detectives Grijpstra and DeGier.

The brilliant creations of

Janwillem van de Wetering

Catch up on all their adventures!
Use the coupon below to order!